ADDITIONAL PRAISE FOR
Further News of Defeat

"Michael X. Wang's debut collection is a masterful amalgam of heart, brutality, and irony. Wang sees deeply into his subject. With offhand precision, his stories present a vision of recent China that feels utterly genuine even when he is raucously, indubitably inventing. This is political fiction of a high caliber."

SHARON SOLWITZ author of *Once, in Lourdes*

"Michael X. Wang's *Further News of Defeat* is a collection of deeply researched and engrossing, wonderfully evocative and moving short stories about the people of a particular village in China and the migration of their descendants to urban centers and new lands. What's extraordinary about this book is how it also reads like a distilled epic, bringing to life the great clash of tradition and progress in a half-century of dizzyingly rapid change in the world's most populous country. A beautiful, assured, and unforgettable debut."

PORTER SHREVE author of *The End of the Book*

"Although the stories in this engrossing debut collection cover myriad perspectives, time periods, and themes, *Further News of Defeat* also reads with the cohesiveness and urgency of the best political novels, capturing the consequences of history's largest, cruelest forces—war, poverty, corruption—on the individual lives of its characters. As the collection weaves through the history of China—both real and imagined—Wang tackles dark, painful subjects with startling tenderness and care. *Further News of Defeat* is a stunning debut from a major new talent."

JAKE WOLFF author of *The History o*

Further News of Defeat

STORIES

Michael X. Wang

AUTUMN
HOUSE PRESS

Grateful acknowledgment is made to the journals where some of these stories first appeared: "New Work in New China" appeared in *The Greensboro Review*, Fall 2019; "Further News of Defeat" appeared in *New England Review*, Winter 2015, and was selected as a notable story of the year for *The Best American Short Stories Anthology* in 2016; "Where Clouds Rain Pearls" appeared in *Cimarron Review*, Fall 2015; "At This Moment, in This Space" appeared in *Juked*, Spring 2015; "A Family Accident" appeared in *Drafthorse*, Winter 2014; "The Whole Story of a Tugboat Driver on Suzhou River" appeared in *Cha: An Asian Literary Journal*, July 2014; "The Well" appeared in *Prick of the Spindle*, December 2013; "A Minor Revolution" appeared in *Day One*, December 2013; "With Consideration and Care" was a 2010 AWP Intro Journals Winner in Fiction and appeared in *Hayden's Ferry Review*, Fall/Winter 2010.

"Autumn House Press" and "Autumn House" are registered trademarks owned by Autumn House Press, a nonprofit corporation whose mission is the publication and promotion of poetry and other fine literature.

Autumn House Press receives state arts funding support through a grant from the Pennsylvania Council on the Arts, a state agency funded by the Commonwealth of Pennsylvania, and the National Endowment for the Arts, a federal agency.

ISBN: 978-1-938769-64-1
Library of Congress Control Number: 2020932436

Cover art: Wang Gai, "Landscape after Ma Yuan" (detail) in the *Mustard Seed Garden Manual of Painting*, 1679; courtesy of The Metropolitan Museum of Art, New York.
Book & cover design: Joel W. Coggins

All Autumn House books are printed on acid-free paper and meet the international standards of permanent books intended for purchase by libraries.

FOR MY FAMILY

Contents

A MINOR REVOLUTION   3

WITH CONSIDERATION AND CARE   24

FURTHER NEWS OF DEFEAT   45

THE WELL   61

CURES AND SUPERSTITIONS   76

THE WHOLE STORY OF A TUGBOAT DRIVER ON SUZHOU RIVER   96

A FAMILY ACCIDENT   106

WHERE CLOUDS RAIN PEARLS   122

AT THIS MOMENT, IN THIS SPACE   140

NEW WORK IN NEW CHINA   152

ACKNOWLEDGMENTS   177

ABOUT THE AUTHOR   179

Further News of Defeat

A MINOR REVOLUTION

When economics professor Zhou Peng told his wife, Shen, that he was joining his students in the hunger strike, she begged him to reconsider, to think of Weiwei, their four-year-old son. Each morning for a week, she rode her bicycle through the crowded Beijing streets, dropping Weiwei off at his preschool before making her way to Tiananmen Square, where protestors gathered around a white obelisk: the Monument to the People's Heroes. She offered her husband plastic bags filled with steamed buns and pickled turnips, but he only accepted the canteens of green tea. "The tea will help my mind stay clear," he said, "so that my body forgets the hunger."

On the morning of June 3, 1989, after hours of pushing and shoving to try to find her husband, she ran into one of his students, a girl named Mumin Sha, who told her that Professor Zhou had been taken the night before. He had been pulled down from the obelisk by three officers carrying batons.

Shen followed Mumin to the police station. A group of students were gathered there as well, waving miniature Chinese flags behind gridiron fences. Among them, a man sat atop the shoulders of another man, shouting into a bullhorn, "Remember the martyrs! Remember Hu Yaobang!" On the other side, officers brandished full-size flags affixed to wooden poles with speared ends. When Shen and Mumin came near the building, their eyes started to water from the lingering pepper spray. Only after they held up their hands to show that they were unarmed did the lead officer allow them to pass through.

Inside the station, Shen and Mumin sat in line behind five women and three men. Two of the men were handcuffed, cupping their palms around dry, crumbling blocks of instant noodles. An officer came from behind the counter with a form for Shen.

"Don't let them know you're his wife," Mumin whispered. "They might use that to their advantage, force Professor Zhou to do things he doesn't want to do."

Shen stared at the form, the metallic pen heavy in her hand. She wanted to cry.

"What's the matter?" Mumin asked. "I'm sorry. That was a stupid thing to say—asking a woman what's wrong when her husband's in jail."

"It's not that." Shen lowered her head. "I don't know how to read."

Mumin paused. Then she reached over for the form. "Don't worry about a thing," she said. "I'll fill it out for you. I have the perfect alias. You are my older sister, and you want to know why this bourgeois-loving intellectual, this evil Zhou Peng, would want to jeopardize my college career by having his class join the protests."

Shen watched the girl write and felt more than ever a sense that she was letting her husband down. She was from the countryside, from a village north of the Yellow River, famous for its fruit-tree commune. Seven years ago, when Zhou Peng had come to her village to update the irrigation system, she'd been nineteen and he, thirty-eight. She was impressed by his dedication, by his power to command all the men in the village, and by his sensitivity. He recited poetry from memory when occasion called for it. She didn't think she'd be able to stimulate him when they moved to Beijing. She told him she couldn't read or write, but he said her illiteracy only made him love her more. "You are the water that sifts through my sand," he said. "Our child will come out of your womb like clay, able to be molded into a perfect Buddha."

She worked hard to fit into the city. It took her a year to learn how to dress and walk like the city folk, a year more to lose her provincial accent, and when Zhou remarked one day at the Red Bridge Fish Market that he couldn't pick her out among the crowd, she felt both proud and ashamed at how much she'd changed. City folk couldn't spot her bumpkin-ness immediately, but an offhand reference or a sheet of paper was all it took to reveal her.

The officer behind the counter took the form, read it, and smiled. He had tiny pigeon eyes and gray sideburns that shot out from under his cap. "Zhou Peng hasn't been mistreated," he said. "Take as long as you need. No one will be watching you."

He led them to a room with a dim overhead lamp and a splintered square table. Zhou Peng sat on the chair farthest from the door, his elbows resting on several sheets of paper, his arms and legs handcuffed. There was a bruise below his receding hairline. Seeing her husband like this, Shen couldn't control herself anymore. She covered her mouth with her hand.

"I don't understand you," she said. "What good does any of this do?"

"Everything will be fine. These things"—her husband shook his arms and legs—"they don't mean anything. The police aren't after me. Anyone standing on top of that monument would've been arrested. Besides, most of the police are sympathetic. They're only following orders." He turned to Mumin. "By the way, how did you get them to let you in?"

Mumin smiled. "I wrote down that we were sisters."

"Smart—just in case the officers lose sympathy." He turned back to his wife. "Not that they will."

"I'll leave you two alone." Mumin got up, squeezed Shen's shoulders, and tapped on the window above the door. The officer glanced inside before letting Mumin out.

"You need to eat something," Shen told her husband. "Look at your wrists: thin as a schoolboy's." She reached into her pocket and took out a half-dozen sesame seed rice balls. "Here, eat this."

Zhou shook his head. "If I eat now, I'll have made worthless the sacrifices of everyone in the hunger strike."

"What difference does it make?" Shen said. "No one can see you. Who would know?"

"*I* would."

"Please. Would you have Weiwei go hungry too if it meant your sacrifice would not be in vain? If you die, that's exactly what will happen. Maybe if you just apologize, the police will let you go."

"Shen." He leaned forward and began talking slower, as if she were one of his students. "I am doing this out of my concern for Weiwei's future and the country he will grow up in. My actions today will be a major victory, as significant as the Red Army's Long March."

She nodded, but the truth was she didn't understand how abstaining from food could ever change the country. During the Great Leap Forward, for the span of a month, she and her parents had survived on nothing but water and wood bark. They hadn't achieved anything, unless mild cholera could be considered an achievement.

"Shen," her husband said. "I want you to leave Beijing. I want you to go back to your parents in the countryside until things here return to normal. Take Weiwei with you. Keep him safe. Tell him his father is overseas in Japan, buying him a color TV."

"No, I'm not leaving. I'm visiting you every morning and bringing you food until you're hungry enough to eat."

"This is no time to be stubborn," her husband said. "Listen to me. Buy two bus tickets and disappear with Weiwei tonight."

She got up as if she hadn't heard him. Leaving the rice balls on the table, she tapped on the window above the door, and again the officer with the pigeon eyes stuck his head in.

"All done?" he said.

"Sit down!" Zhou shouted. "Shen, I'm not done talking to you yet."

"I'll be back tomorrow to bring you breakfast." She nodded to the officer, who kept the door open until she walked out. Only a minor rebellion, she thought. It wasn't enough for her husband to stop loving her, just as his hunger strike wasn't enough for her to stop loving him.

"When will they let him out?" Shen shouted to Mumin, who was pedaling in front of her. They were on their way to the new spot Zhou's students had picked out.

"From the looks of it, maybe a week or two," Mumin shouted back. "They're keeping him there to prevent him from causing more trouble. Once the protest ends, they'll let him go."

"Are you sure? What if they don't?"

"Standing on the obelisk is not a crime. They pulled him down and put him in prison to scare the rest of us. But they don't know that we aren't scared."

They locked their bicycles in front of the Great Hall of the People, its columns casting long shadows the students huddled under. Across the street, old veterans, wearing green shorts and carrying string pianos and Chinese violins, played "March of the People's Volunteer Army," a marching tune made famous during the Korean War. Mumin stepped onto a wooden platform, and another student handed her a bullhorn.

"Professor Zhou is locked in prison!" Mumin shouted to her classmates. "He tells us to remain strong! Just like us, he will continue to fast! The government doesn't want blood on their hands, and they will soon listen to our pleas!"

After Mumin had finished her speech, Shen swung her legs around her bicycle and rode through the crowds to her son's preschool.

Weiwei sat on the steel rod connecting the bicycle seat to the handlebars. Every few minutes, he reached into his trousers and then smelled his fingers, upsetting the bicycle's balance. Shen was sure he had defecated in his pants again.

"When did you do it?" she asked. "Morning or afternoon?"

The boy glanced up, innocent. "I didn't do anything."

"So when we get home, I won't find any surprises?"

The boy's lips curled to reveal two missing teeth. "Maybe a very small one."

"When did you lose your second front tooth?"

"This morning," he said. "I buried it under a tree. My teacher told me it'll help the tree grow."

Shen saved all her son's teeth in a used bamboo-preserve jar. Whenever she was bored, she'd take it out, shake it, and listen to its rattling, trying to imagine what her son was doing that very moment. Her grandmother in the village had done the same. She'd told

Shen that if you could hear a part of someone's body making a noise, it meant that person could still speak, and if he could still speak, he was still alive.

"You should've given it to me," she said. "There are enough trees in the world, but there's only one of you."

Back home, after cleaning out Weiwei's pants and setting them above the rusted heater to dry, she boiled two eggs and opened a can of snow peas. She resteamed the buns she had tried giving Mumin and the other students that morning, and as she scolded Weiwei for spitting out his egg yolk and playing with his food, she watched from her window the hordes of people gathering around Tiananmen Square. Their one-room apartment, provided by the university, was on the second floor of a ten-story building, the Forbidden City looming a few blocks in front of it like a series of increasingly complex mazes. Below her window, students yelled up, "Join the protests! Never forget Hu Yaobang!"

Who was this Hu Yaobang? Her husband had talked to his students about him, but he never bothered explaining the man's importance to *her*. She didn't understand what everybody wanted from the government. They shouted about change and reform, but when she asked them *what* needed to be changed and reformed, none of them could give her a real answer. They told her, "Our voices have to be heard," which sounded ridiculous to her. Wasn't it apparent that everyone could hear them already?

To her, China was improving. The people on TV said so, and her own experiences mirrored what they said. Her parents didn't go hungry anymore, new buildings shot up every other month, and the theaters started showing foreign movies. What more did people want? It was like what her father had always said: nobody could eat enough to grow fat in a day.

Weiwei wanted to watch TV. Shen turned on their twelve-inch

black-and-white Panasonic and went to the sink to boil water for his bath. When the pot started steaming, she poured it into a basin with a cartoon panda imprint and added two liters of lukewarm water from the tap. Weiwei stripped, gleefully touching the tip of his penis.

"Look how big I can get it," he said.

She laughed. "As big as your father's," she said. "And you've grown whiskers." She lathered the melon-scented soap on his face and scrubbed away the streaks of dirt above his upper lip.

After tucking Weiwei into bed, she turned down the TV. She watched the news coverage for half an hour, listening for her husband's name. Then she turned it off and lay next to Weiwei, staring out her window at the people holding flashlights and candles—blips of illumination like the fireflies that came to her village during the summer.

In truth, she wouldn't mind living with her parents again, away from this important city, these important people, and these important things that were happening. But she equated leaving Zhou in prison to leaving him in a grave. She was sure he needed her more than he was letting on.

Outside, she heard a distant rumbling. The chopsticks shook in the drawer and the overhead light, hanging from a metal chain, swung back and forth. Half a mile away, behind the swirling blue of police cars, she could see the first of the tanks lining up.

The next morning, Shen returned to the police station. The officer with the pigeon eyes recognized her. "I know who you are," he said, "but you don't need to be afraid. Your husband is safe." He brought her to the same room from the day before. "Take as long as you need."

"Shen, sit down." Her husband's voice was dry and raspy, as if he'd slept in the Gobi Desert. His face was dirty, and Shen could barely make out the bruise from the day before. "Now you have to listen to me. I heard the tanks. With the army in the city, nobody is safe anymore."

"Least of all you," Shen said.

Her husband didn't say anything.

Shen, feeling proud that she'd stumped him, took out a bowl of rice porridge and set it, along with a pair of chopsticks, on the splintered table. "Eat."

"How about a truce," her husband said. "I'll make you a deal. If I eat half of this bowl, you leave the city. Does that sound fair?"

Shen shook her head. "You eat the entire bowl, and tomorrow morning, before I get on the bus, I'll bring you another bowl, and you eat that too. Fair?"

Frowning, her husband reached for the chopsticks. "I've never seen you like this. Forget what I said. You're not water. We're a pair of rocks, colliding into each other like two boulders trying to sharpen the same needle. Before long, nothing will remain between our surfaces."

Shen was relieved and excited by her victory over her husband and seeing that she still had a few hours before she had to pick up Weiwei, rode her bicycle over to the Great Hall of the People, hoping that she'd be able to convince Mumin and the other students to eat as well. She knew from personal experience what being hungry felt like, and it wouldn't be long before they'd give in to the sweet aroma of freshly steamed buns.

Arriving at the wooden platform, she was surprised to see the students celebrating. They were holding each other's hands and lifting their knuckles in the air, congratulating one another on their perseverance. Even Mumin, the bullhorn hanging from her belt, shed tears of joy.

"What's going on?" Shen asked.

"Didn't you hear? They're pulling out. As we speak, the tanks are turning around and leaving the city. Even the army is on our side!"

Shen saw this as a chance to bring up food. "What great news," she said. "We should celebrate. Which reminds me: I've brought something from home."

"Oh, no," Mumin said. "Now is not the time to eat. We have them in a corner. It won't be long before they ask for a meeting." She took Shen's hands. "You should join us. I see the spirit of the revolution in you."

The girl's fingers were thin and cold with barely the strength of a cicada. "No, I won't be of any help," Shen said. "I can't read, and my husband would never agree." She was careful not to give the real reason: she didn't believe in their cause.

"That's not true. Professor Zhou would love nothing more than to see his wife join him in the protest."

Shen stared at Mumin. For the first time since meeting the girl, she felt smarter. She was sure the girl had never experienced love before. The girl had probably never been in a relationship. The girl didn't understand, as she herself did, that no man as good as her husband would ever risk the things most important to him.

"Sorry," Shen said. "I have to pick up my son."

By the time she returned home, a gang of students wearing white headbands was on her street. Drunk, they threw flaming bottles of wine at her building, heaving them as high as the third-floor balconies. "Come out, students!" they shouted. "Join the others!" Shen hid in an alleyway, clutching Weiwei to her chest, until the students moved on to the next university housing unit. Soon, the police arrived, but the students ran off before they could be arrested.

Upstairs, an officer hosed down her balcony. He picked up a half-burned bedsheet and handed her a scallion plant, a chunk of clay blasted off the pot. "Looks like only minor damage," the officer said. "Use the public phone if you see them again." He tipped his head and left.

As Shen swept the ash off the balcony, Weiwei poked his head out and asked what happened.

"Just some teenagers playing with fireworks," Shen said. "Go inside and fill up your bath basin."

"I want to watch TV."

"Go inside or you won't get a banana after dinner."

She didn't know whether to be irritated or proud that Weiwei was as stubborn as his father. So far, the hunger strike had only blackened the bedcover her mother had given her. Watching too much TV, Shen imagined, would blacken Weiwei's mind, leaving him as illiterate as she was.

Sometimes she blamed herself for his attachment to the TV. She wished she could read to him. A few months ago, Weiwei had exited his preschool waving a letter his teacher wrote saying what a good student he was. He wanted her to read it right then, but she managed to convince him to bring it to his father so they could read it together. That night, when Zhou read the letter with a chicken bone in his mouth, she was filled with envy and became convinced that one day Weiwei would love his father more. Once he entered grade school, he'd know there was something wrong with her. He'd grow up embarrassed, being the only one among his friends whose mother couldn't tell the difference between the character for music and the one for parrot. And she'd be ashamed for him, too.

Something flashed in the corner of her eye. She was about to go inside and tell Weiwei to turn off the TV, but realized the flash had come from the opposite direction. Squinting, she saw more flashes, then heard cracking sounds. She stood up, gaining just enough vision to peer over buildings and see soldiers shooting into groups of students. Suddenly, a jeep caught fire, and for a moment, the night lit up like the eve of the Spring Festival.

"Weiwei!" She ran inside. "Where are you!"

"Here." Naked, the boy wobbled out of the bathroom carrying the water-filled basin.

"Drop that! We need to leave."

"Where are we going?"

"To see Baba. Quickly now, put on your clothes."

Shen wrapped a sweater over his shoulders as the boy zipped up his shorts. If one could hear the death of others, she believed, it was only a matter of time before one heard one's own.

Down on the street, she was surprised that almost everyone else was calm. A crowd gathered on the other side, listening to the sounds from several blocks down the hill. Two old men played chess. A couple shared binoculars and aimed them between buildings. "Senseless city folks," Shen muttered. She set Weiwei on the handlebar and swung her legs around the bicycle seat.

The officer with the pigeon eyes yelled that she was lucky he noticed her tonight. Otherwise they'd probably arrest her, too. He wouldn't let her past the gridiron fence that hundreds of protestors were pressed against. Some were trampled to the ground, and students carried bodies to the rickshaws, whose drivers then sped in the direction of the nearest hospitals. Weiwei stared at everything, and several times Shen had to yank his hand with more force than she wanted to get him to keep walking. The gunfire was off in the distance, but she heard rumors among the crowd that the army was coming this way, the police station a valuable site to keep clear of protestors.

"Let me in for a moment!" Shen shouted. "Just to know he's alive!"

A woman next to Shen nodded fiercely. "Yeah, let the woman see her husband!"

"Look around," the officer said. He stood shoulder-to-shoulder with other officers, forming a second fence. "Does it look like anyone is getting through?"

"Baba is in prison?" Weiwei asked.

"Just a peek," Shen said. "Won't you do me this last favor?"

Three blocks down, smoke appeared from an alleyway. A dozen students were running away from that direction, their shirts stretched to cover their faces. "Soldiers!" one of them shouted. A mob rushed over to join them, pushing taxis, vendor carts, and traffic signs onto the street and forming a barricade to delay the army.

The officer wiggled down and leaned close to Shen's cheeks. For a second, she thought he might kiss her. "I can vouch for the professor's safety," he whispered. "Now go. For heaven's sake, you have a kid with you."

Shen nodded, then shoved her way out of the crowd. A protestor was about to snap off her bicycle's chains with pliers and throw her bicycle onto the barricade, but stopped when Shen ran over waving her arms. She wanted to thank the man for not taking her vehicle, but she was sure if she tried saying anything, she'd cry.

She pedaled west on Second Ring Road to the Gate of Virtuous Triumph. The bus stop was just outside the gate, and if she remembered correctly, the last one left at eleven.

"I don't feel good." Weiwei hugged his elbow to his stomach. "My belly hurts."

"I'm sorry," she said. "Try to ignore it."

"Are you crying?" Weiwei glanced up, rubbing the spot where his teeth used to be with his tongue. "The police said Baba was all right."

She tried to smile. "I know, little devil. How about we go see Grandma tonight? You like Grandma?"

"Yeah," Weiwei said. "And that means we get to ride the bus!" The boy's favorite cartoon was *The Transformers*. Shen knew his dream was to one day drive a car.

"Yes." She laughed. "We'll ride it for the entire night!"

Second Ring Road was nearly empty on this side of the city, away from the busy mausoleum. Ambulances, three-wheeled taxis, and rickshaws were all heading in the direction opposite of Tiananmen Square, and the few bicyclers alongside Shen pedaled with leisure, their feet moving slowly, resting when going down a hill, as if the night were like any other. Shen cursed her husband for what he'd done. If he'd only listened to her and apologized to the police, they'd be like all these other people on the street, coming home from work or the market or dinner with friends.

Three blocks from the gate, she saw a woman on the other side of the road walking by a fried dough stand. The bullhorn on her belt reflected the glow of the lamppost, and by her height and figure, the woman might have been Mumin Sha. Shen rode a few meters forward, glanced back, and convinced now that the girl was in fact Zhou's student, crossed the street.

"Mumin!" Shen shouted.

The girl stopped, turned to look at Shen, and then lowered her head. She smelled faintly of gasoline. There was a black handprint on her blouse, and her hair was matted with sweat.

"What happened?" Shen asked. "Why are you here?"

"There," Mumin said, putting her hand over her mouth. "There."

She pointed in the direction of the Forbidden City.

Shen reached over and cupped the girl's wrists. "It's all right. We're in a safe part of town. Listen. We can't hear the rifles anymore." Shen was talking slower now, the way her husband would sometimes speak to her. Mumin would be used to this manner of speech. Shen guided her to a nearby bench, and gave Weiwei some money to buy two egg-wrapped fried dough sticks. "Do you remember the first time we met, how we pretended we were sisters? Now, start from the beginning. Tell your older sister what happened."

"We were wrong." Mumin blew her nose into the handkerchief Shen gave her. "The tanks weren't leaving. They were regrouping." The girl explained how the army got through their road barriers, ramming them with plow trucks before sending in the infantry. The soldiers shot canisters of tear gas, and when the students still didn't leave, began firing live bullets. "Two of us got hit, and instead of helping, the others just ran. I stayed as long as I could, until the rickshaws picked them up. Then I ran, too. I remembered what Professor Zhou had told us to do if things got bad and headed east for the bus station."

"You didn't do anything wrong," Shen said. "You shouldn't be ashamed."

Weiwei came back with two sticks of fried dough. Shen ripped one in half, gave it to her son, and handed the rest to Mumin. The girl wolfed down the smaller stick in one bite, a chunk of it swelling up in her throat as she swallowed.

Weiwei laughed. "Ma, your little sister must be hungry!"

Shen took out a thermos from her handbag. "Drink this," she said. "Eat slowly. All of it is yours."

Mumin stared at the fried dough. "I wouldn't have done it," she said, shaking her head. "I wouldn't have done it if I'd have known."

"Not even Professor Zhou knew."

"Professor Zhou!" The girl shot up. "I almost forgot. He's still in prison. We need to go back!"

Shen pulled the girl down. "I was just there. It's too dangerous. Professor Zhou cares about you, just as he cares about me and Wei-wei, and he wouldn't want us to do anything that would put our lives in any more danger."

The girl hugged Shen. "He is a good man."

Shen nodded. "But too stubborn."

There was a long line at the Gate of Virtuous Triumph. Two officers stood under the gate, questioning the people at the front. Behind them was a parked jeep with a machine gun turret. At the top of the ancient gate, in between the battlements, a soldier shined down a searchlight. The red moon, covered by smoke that drifted up from Tiananmen Square, appeared to Shen like a partly eaten peach.

Half a block from the gate, she pointed to the bullhorn on Mumin's belt and told her to throw it away. Mumin loosened the strap and threw it on the grass.

"Maybe we should go back," the girl said.

Shen shook her head. "We don't have anywhere to go. They'll look for us at the housing units. Come to my village. It's a hundred kilometers west of the city. Stay for a few months, until things return to normal. Nobody will look for us there."

"I feel like a coward."

"The dead don't understand bravery."

Shen pushed her bicycle to the end of the line. There was yelling coming from the front. She stood on her toes and, over the shoulders of those in front of her, saw a man and a woman being pulled out of the line and to the side.

"My belly really hurts," Weiwei said, kneading his stomach. "I have to poo."

A soldier escorted the couple into the jeep, where there were several other citizens. Shen turned and stared at Weiwei.

"You want me to find him a bathroom?" Mumin asked.

"No," Shen said. "Go in your pants, Weiwei. Don't be afraid."

The boy looked at Mumin and then at Shen. "Really?"

"Yeah," Shen said. "Make it as dirty as you can."

"There's no need for the boy to suffer. Really, it wouldn't be too much trouble."

"It's all right." Shen smiled, patting her son on the back.

By the time they reached the front, the people before and after them had noticed the smell. The officers let the couple before them through after the couple told them that their son had run away and they were looking for him outside Beijing. When it was Shen's turn, Mumin came up to the officers and smiled.

"My sister's from the countryside and she's visiting Beijing," she told them. "You see, I've never seen my nephew before."

The officer shined a flashlight in her face. The second officer whispered something to the first officer. Then the first officer started shining the light down Mumin's body.

"You're so dirty," he said. "What's your occupation? Are you a student?"

Mumin froze.

Shen stepped forward holding Weiwei. Immediately the flashlight fell on her. "Please, officers." She spoke using her village accent. "We're in a hurry. My son went in his pants, and we need to clean his trousers before his bottom starts to swell. There's a bathroom right next to the bus station. If you want, you can watch me clean."

The officer leaned in, focusing the flashlight on Weiwei.

"Don't believe me?" She held Weiwei up to the officer's face.

Both officers took a step back. Pinching their noses, they waved Shen and Mumin through.

On the bus, a smirk began to form on Mumin's face. The two women turned and stared at each other. Shen was the first to burst out laughing. Patting Weiwei on the head, she peered out the window. Beijing's lights were growing dimmer, the smoke had cleared, and the only outside sound was the wind blowing through her window's slits.

Two weeks later, at the village, she received a letter without a return address. It was from Professor Zhou, Mumin said. She took out the letter and began to read:

Dear Water,

I don't know if you'll find someone to read this. It's been hard in here. The police told me the protests are over, but I can't be sure. I've given them a few names, and they promised to reduce my sentence. They never told me how long it had been originally, but a Party lawyer said afterward that it wouldn't be more than three years. I'm a political prisoner, and visitors aren't allowed now.

I know you are smart, I know Weiwei is safe, and I know they won't find you in the village. Don't be sad. Think of my time away as an extended academic trip. When I called you from Singapore and Vietnam and North Korea, I would always recite you a poem, and I will do so now:

The firecracker's sound brings in the new year,

The spring wind warms the house,

On the eve of a happy occasion,

Everyone looks forward to the morning sun.

Mumin handed the letter to Shen, who put it into the used bamboo-preserve jar. Later that night, she only told Weiwei about the poem. Three years, she thought. Weiwei would be seven, barely in grade school. Zhou would be out before his son grew up.

On TV, she and Mumin watched the protests being dispersed around the country, shots of youths being handcuffed, their parents weeping, empty plazas littered with leaflets, stools, and plastic bags. Shen thought back to the day when the tanks had left, and it occurred to her that if the students would have just taken their victory and returned home, none of them would be dead. They might even have become heroes. Her grandfather had been a gambler, and he said the most difficult thing about gambling was knowing when you'd won enough.

Everyone in the village expressed how sorry they were about what had happened to her husband, about how Weiwei would have fewer opportunities now. Shen would nod, but in her heart, she knew the opposite. She understood the village and knew how to help her son. Even if Zhou never returned, Weiwei would grow up with something to strive toward: leaving the countryside and returning to the city of his father. At the very least, the other boys at school wouldn't make fun of him—chances were good that their mothers couldn't read either.

She felt comfortable not having to pretend anymore. Just the other day, her mother, kneading a loaf of sorghum bread, told her about the election for a new village chief. *An election!* Shen thought. *Progress was being made!* There were two candidates to choose from: one who gave each household a dozen eggs and another who hauled a kilo of flour to every yard. Her mother told Shen to go to the town square and vote for the one who gave them the flour. When it was Shen's turn in line, she grabbed three kidney beans—one for her mother, another for her son, the third for herself—and threw them into the bucket with the picture of the flour-hauler. Afterward, she and her friends chatted about who they had picked. "I tossed my bean into egg-man's bucket because my son loves hard-boiled eggs," one of her friends said. "But a kilo of flour is worth much more," another added. "All of your reasons are bad," Shen said, grinning. "I chose out of filial duty. I picked the one my mother wanted me to." They all laughed.

In the morning, Mumin helped out at the village high school, and at night, she gave Weiwei private lessons. On occasion, Shen would lean over and learn a few words herself.

Inside her family's adobe hut, she was amazed that she'd forgotten how loud the crickets chirped. She chewed on a dried apple slice, pulling the torn bedcover through a sewing machine, a rapid *tat-tat-tat* filling the room.

"I can't hear Teacher Sha's voice," Weiwei said.

He was sitting on the stone bed with Mumin. A history book was on his lap and a notebook was in his hand. His grandmother was sleeping behind them.

"Oh, I'm sorry," Shen said.

Mumin took the book off Weiwei's lap. "Go show your mother the new character you learned to write."

The boy inched off the bed, leapt down, and made his way over. Then he held out the notebook in front of his face.

Shen stitched another line before turning and squinting at the pad. On it there was a poorly written character. The bottom part, she believed, was too big compared to the top and contained an extra line.

"It's *pao*," Weiwei said. His hand made the shape of a pistol, glancing back at Mumin for approval. "*Pao!*" he repeated, "the character for cannon."

Shen studied the word, and nodded. Her son returned to his lesson. Shen lifted the sewn-up bedcover, the light shining through it and revealing the stitches, and she was reassured, despite and maybe because of her husband's absence, at how simple the world felt again.

WITH CONSIDERATION AND CARE

Others in line carried tins of moon cake and sequined bottles of rice wine. Fu held a plastic bag. It contained three ripe tangerines and an inexpensive box of coconut rolls. Fu was certain, when his name was called, that the family-planning commissioner would not be sympathetic to his case.

"Fu Yung Ji?" the man said, taking out several sheets of paper. On one of them, Fu saw a picture of himself, tinged red and stamped with the five yellow stars of China. "It says here you want to marry your daughter. Is this true?"

"Oh, no, you have it all wrong," Fu said, and then stopped himself. "What I mean is, if your honor would look things over again, you would see that she was never my daughter. I never adopted her."

The commissioner reached for his glasses. He examined Fu's document without putting them on. He read quickly, the lenses hovering above the paper. "*Lin Hong, born August 1990 in Fenyang, China, went to New York, United States of America with parents in 1992, deported to China in 1999 after death of parents, entrusted to Fu Yung Ji of Xinchun Village through her parents' will.*" He stopped. "Well," he said. "The key word here is entrusted. It could mean many things."

"But certainly, your honor, entrusted can't mean adopted."

"Don't be so quick to make judgments, Fu." The commissioner untied the plastic bag, took out a tangerine, and started peeling it. "Delicious," he said, leaning back in his chair. "The committee meets every month to discuss delicate issues like this. It's fortunate for you that it just finished its deliberations two days ago. Now, I'll have more time to think about the matter. A word like entrusted could be interpreted in a variety of ways."

It was true, Fu considered, that Lin's parents had thought of him as family—her father had been an orphan at Xinchun and was raised by Fu's parents (Fu was their only child; they needed the extra hand in the fields)—but could such connections prevent him from marrying her? "Is there anything I could do," he said, "to strengthen my case?"

"Your case is rather odd. It's as if you want to marry not only your daughter but also your niece." The commissioner laughed, browsing through the pages. "You should write up a report. Explain to me in detail why you think the two of you should wed." The commissioner snapped his chair back down and popped a slice of tangerine into his mouth. "And Fu," he said, "next time, bring more than just oranges."

The club had just opened. Lin Hong had seen it advertised on buses. There was a picture of a white man dancing, his hair the color of hay. Beneath him, the caption read: "A taste of the other side! We guarantee one dancing American every night!"

Lin was shivering. The bus from Xinchun Village to Yuncheng

City took an hour, and in order to conserve gas, it was never heated. The line to the club took another hour. Snow fell in chunks, landing on her hair like cotton. With one hand, she held down her scarf and with the other, she linked arms with her best friend, Yan.

"I don't even know why you're here," Yan said. "You're already an American."

Lin laughed, frost escaping her lips. "Yeah, but now the owner can brag that he has *two* dancing Americans tonight."

"I hope the American's a guy, and single."

"Get out of here." Lin shoved her friend's shoulder with her own. "Is that him?"

They saw a tall, dark-haired man wearing a cashmere coat and sunglasses. As he walked past, Lin smelled a trace of cologne. If only her parents hadn't died, she would be in the presence of such men all the time.

"Lin? Yan? I thought it was the two of you." The voice, somehow scary, made them unlink their arms and stop their giggling. They turned around. It was their science teacher, Mr. Nan. He shoved his way into the line, not paying attention to the angry faces of the people behind him. He was young, a recent graduate of Shanxi University. Lin would have considered him handsome, except for his short height and the large black spots on his neck—a sulfuric acid accident, he had explained on the first day of class.

"You girls shouldn't be out this late at night."

"Yes, Mr. Nan," they said, almost in unison.

"I'm kidding." He laughed. He took his hand out of his pocket and gave Lin an awkward pat on the arm. "So, you girls like hip-hop?"

They looked at each other.

"Yeah, me too. Of course, I couldn't have told you this in class, but I was a bebopper in college. I know a little break dancing, and I love techno." He sounded out the last word: TE – CH – NO. "Do you girls like techno?"

Yan started to nod, but Lin shook her head.

"Of course, I also like the Beijing opera—I watch it with my parents—if you girls like that sort of thing."

Lin thought about Fu, who was probably at home watching the opera at this very moment. When she was with her father—no, not her father, Fu never let her call him that—he would listen while smoking a pipe, either sitting down, his legs crossed, or pacing around the yard, his arms locked behind his back. She remembered the time when she came home early from school and found him listening in his same way to her Mariah Carey CD. He told her that his opera CDs were scratched. He had been embarrassed, deeply so, although he was embarrassed about everything.

"But I never got to live my dream of being a professional bebopper." Mr. Nan's arms were crossed, like he didn't know what to do with them. "I don't always want to be a high school science teacher, you know. I got plans in the works to leave this place forever."

A conniver, full of plans, just like Fu. Too scared to face problems head-on. Always looking for a back door. She never knew where Fu went, what he thought about all day. During the off-season, such as winter, when there was nothing much to be done in the fields, she would still come home and find the front yard empty. He might be a frequenter of brothels—the reason he was always telling her how poor they were.

"That's really interesting, Mr. Nan." Lin re-slung her scarf around her neck and grabbed Yan's hand. "Looks like the line's moving. Perhaps we'll see each other on the dance floor."

"I'd like that," he said. "And if you girls ever do something like this again, give me a call. Don't hesitate. I'm not a teacher when we're not in class."

The bouncer stepped aside to let the girls in. When Mr. Nan stepped forward, the bouncer held out his hand and re-linked the security chain.

Fu cut his finger while chopping scallions. He was going to surprise her when she got home. Lamb and carrot dumplings were Lin's favorite. Now the dish was spoiled, his blood dripping into the egg yoke as he tried dumping the knifeful of scallion into the mixing bowl. There was no other way to put it: he was getting old. Both his parents had had arthritis. And now, at fifty-two, Fu was finding it difficult to stand for more than an hour or two. Lying in bed at night, he would cup his hands above his kneecap and tug at them, seeing how far they would extend. He sucked on his finger and tried to chop the rest of the scallions using one hand, but then his legs started to shake. Strange, he thought, how one pain would lead to another, like pulling a shoelace.

He sat down and took out a piece of paper. A report, to strengthen his case. What could he put down? He had been a young widower, lost his wife when she was twenty-five to a cholera epidemic. He had held her shriveled body during the last stages, her cheeks hollowed-out from sickness. Twelve people died that year in Xinchun due to the epidemic. He attended the mass funeral. A government official had handed him and the others an apology and a bouquet of cherry blossoms before driving off in his jeep. That same year, Lin came to Fu from America, nine years old and also aware of death. The sole survivor of a car accident, she often had dreams about being in the upside-down station wagon, staring at the shards of windshield in her dad's ear while waiting for the police to arrive.

The other villagers had congratulated him. "Look at how Old Man in Heaven takes care of you," they said. "He knows a man as young as you shouldn't be alone." Fu understood what they meant, but as early as that moment, he had the vague fantasy of raising the pretty, full-cheeked girl and marrying her.

He didn't take these thoughts seriously until a week ago, when he saw a dead rabbit in the snows of his sorghum fields. He had bent down to look at it, his elbows touching his knees, and he could tell that it had once been majestic. Its fur was white and its eyes were as red as rusted iron. He realized then that even a creature of such splendor was no match for death if no one was there to take care of it. What would happen to him? He was only human, the most delicate of species, the only one that couldn't preserve its beauty in old age.

"The dead rabbit," he wrote down on the sheet of paper, a new paragraph. Then, thinking better of mentioning the incident, he crossed it out.

Mr. Nan assured them that the cat corpse was well preserved. Lin, Yan, and the other students gathered around Mr. Nan's table, staring at the iodined remains. They sketched and labeled the vital organs, bloodless and purple. It was the second time in a week Lin was forced to see a dead animal. Fu had forced her to help him bury a dead jackrabbit. "But it's disgusting," she'd said. "Look at all the flies. It's not sanitary."

"Someday when you die, would you like it if someone said that about your dead body, how disgusting it was? Or would you like him to take care of you, show you the respect you deserve in death?" They had placed the rabbit on a silk handkerchief, taking it to the old well to be buried. She thought Fu was losing his mind.

More than ever did she feel fortunate that she'd soon be out of high school and old enough to finally leave this man with whom she had no blood connections.

"Doesn't that cat look like my family's cat?" Yan asked.

"I hope not," Lin said. "Otherwise, I won't be able to look at your cat the same way ever again."

"Poor Little Turnip. Be sure to remind me never to let my parents sell him."

"Don't be stupid, Yan. These cats were raised in cages. They probably eat iodine-enriched cat food. They don't just allow us to dissect any cat we want."

Yan nodded. Lin didn't belong in Xinchun. She wasn't a peasant—she knew more than they did. She had come to the village with a photo album and a five-book encyclopedia set—the only things of her parents she had left. In the album, there were moments that she couldn't remember: a picture of her on her father's shoulder, a huge waterfall in the background; another of her in a stroller being pushed by her mother, the photo tinged blue by the aquarium tank where schools of fish were swimming past. Lin felt her English eroding with every passing year at Xinchun, and although she took English as a second language, she could barely make out an encyclopedia entry even with the help of a dictionary.

The bell rang and her classmates were rushing out.

"Ms. Yan and Ms. Lin," Mr. Nan called after them. "Can I speak with the two of you for a moment?"

By his serious tone, Lin thought they were in trouble for talking in class.

"I have some great news," he said, still carrying the cat. His hands were purple. "I found out earlier today that I have been admitted to graduate school in America. My friends and I are planning to go to the new club again this weekend. How would you girls like to come?" They didn't say anything, and he added, "I'm not going to be your teacher for much longer."

Lin watched Yan, shocked by how enthusiastically her friend agreed. This man? Lin thought. Going to the United States?

Fu had to bring it up somehow. But he wanted everything to be perfect. He tried to anticipate all her objections. First, he had to make sure that it was legal, that the family-planning commissioner would approve. He wasn't sure how he would convince the other villagers, though he also believed that they were on his side. After all, she was not his actual daughter. Nor was she a great catch. She was pretty, but the truth was, she scared away prospective suitors by the very fact that she had lived in America. Also, she didn't know how to cook or tend a field. He had spoiled her: She didn't believe she needed to do the manual labor required of a bumpkin wife. From her first moment at Xinchun, Fu had instilled in her this sense of superiority, giving her the largest room in his yard, cooking for her, telling her that she was meant for better things.

Fu scolded himself for not having been harsher with her. He wondered if *he* even wanted her for a wife. How well would she take care of him in his final years? Did he want her around only because he was so used to her? No, he thought, she was still young. There was time to train her. Whatever faults she had could be undone. His first wife didn't even know how to make a bed when they had married, but by the end, she was domesticated enough to dump their morning stool. If she had changed, so would Lin.

He heard the front door slam shut. "The dumplings are almost finished," he called. "Grab the chopsticks and set the table."

"What's the special occasion? The spring festival is still two weeks away." Lin hung her backpack on the polished, Qing-dynasty coatrack Fu's parents had passed down. Then she rested her head on the table.

Fu unhooked a ladle and stirred the dumpling-leek soup. After tasting it for consistency, he added more vinegar. "Get up," he said. "I'm serious. Peel some garlic."

"What's with you, today? So demanding."

"I just feel lucky to have someone like you." Fu took several cloves of garlic, pressed them with a knife, and handed them to Lin.

"I feel lucky as well."

"Why's that?"

"My science teacher is going to America. I'm going to get him to marry me."

He turned around and watched her peel. Since he had pressed the garlic first with a knife, all she had to do was twist her finger and the peels tore off like wings of a cicada. He asked her, "When did you make this decision?"

"No time in particular," she said, though she knew exactly when and where she had decided: today, by the frozen pond, while walking home from school with Yan. It was late February now. The pond froze over every year around December. It would be safe to walk over until the first or second week of March. As they were walking past, Yan was still talking about Mr. Nan and the party at the new club, and she said that it was a "limited opportunity." Lin realized then that if she didn't walk over the pond soon she might have to wait a long time before she got another chance. "But why do *you* feel lucky?" she asked Fu.

He shook his head, glad that the wrinkles on his face were also good at hiding tears. "It was nothing," he said, "I shouldn't have put much hope in it."

That night, like every night, he lay awake in bed, listening to Lin in the other room watching the American channel on CC-TV.

WITH CONSIDERATION AND CARE

The more he thought about the situation, the more worried he got. He remembered a time when she'd listen to whatever he said. One word about wolves lurking in the fields at night and she wouldn't go out past sunset for a month. Why couldn't he convince her of anything now? Why couldn't he have the powers of a father without being her father?

At the club, none of Mr. Nan's friends showed up. Lin questioned whether he even had any. The bouncer didn't let him in until Lin and Yan told him that he was with them. Nan danced awkwardly. He couldn't control his arms and feet at the same time, and his head dangled from his neck like a toy lion during the Spring Festival.

"You wanted to be a bebopper?" Lin shouted over the music.

"It's been a long time since I've danced."

"What about that other night?"

Mr. Nan looked down. The disco-ball lights passed over his face so that Lin couldn't make out the individual spots on his neck or even notice that he had any. He said, "I never got in," and she felt bad for asking.

The three of them danced in a triangle, never daring to move from their corner of the floor. Watching the other dancers, Lin could tell who lived in the city and who came from the countryside. The ones who tended to move around a lot, taking up the entire floor and inching close to other people's backs, they were from the city, confident because it was their home turf. The ones who moved in one place, dancing as if they were on some sort of treadmill, looking around frequently and hoping that no one would notice them, these were the bumpkins, afraid because, in the event of a disagreement, they would always be the ones thrown out first.

She was angry at Nan. Why was *he* so afraid? He'd gone to college, and he was going to America. He should be the most confident man here, except for maybe the American, who was dancing on a large platform in the middle of the floor, girls taking turns being next to him. It was up to her, Lin decided, to show Nan how to be confident, how to uphold himself. After all, a lion with a monkey's brain would not scare a cricket.

On the bus ride home, the girls listened while Nan talked. Unlike in the club, he seemed to be completely at ease in the brightness, where it was just the three of them sitting in the last row. "I got into a zoology program, though I doubt I'll continue in the field. I'll probably transfer to something more practical, like pharmacy."

"That's a good idea," Yan said. Lin could tell she was just agreeing, with no knowledge of *why* it was more practical. She wondered if Nan saw through this, if he bought her act and started liking her friend.

It was past midnight when the bus dropped them off at the village. The three of them walked Yan home first, and afterward, Lin and Nan walked in silence. The village had already started decorating for the Spring Festival. Paper lanterns—red, orange, and green with phoenix and lotus cutouts—hung over doors. Triangles of fortune were plastered on the walls and doormats, and even the old well had "hope" and "life" written on its stones in careful calligraphy.

"When are you leaving?" Lin asked.

"I've been saving up for a plane ticket ever since I sent in my applications." He stopped and turned to her. "But the university already agreed to pay for my ticket, so by the time classes end for Spring Festival recess, I'll have enough money for an additional ticket that I won't need."

She started walking a few steps in front of him, hiding the smile on her face. She was surprised by the suddenness of it all, that he wanted to be with her as much as she him.

"I was thinking," he said, taking small and frequent steps to try and catch up with her. "That if you'd like to come, maybe—"

She slowed down but didn't look at him. She wondered what was the source of his desperation in finding a wife. Not that someone needed to be desperate to want her—she knew boys at school liked her—but Mr. Nan was not a boy, not someone stuck in the village with no means. Could going somewhere new cause as much panic as staying in the same place your entire life?

When he got close enough, she kissed him on the cheek and poked her hand through his arm. They walked like that until they reached her yard. She decided that she'd make the best of this upcoming Spring Festival, since it just might be the last one she'd spend in Xinchun.

Saturday mornings, Fu went to the public baths. This was especially important during the winter, when he wasn't able to turn on the faucet in his yard and shower with the hose. It was also important to reach the baths no later than ten or eleven, as by noon, the water grew so filthy that it did more bad than good. Two baths operated within walking distance: Tang Ming Baths, named after the famous emperor, where the wealthier villagers went, and Nun Min Baths, where the poorer villagers went. There were separate pools for men and women, though children could enter either. Before Lin had turned eleven or twelve, when Fu could no longer convince her to go to the baths with him, he had taken her to Tang Ming's, where the water was soapy and perfumed. She had not been embarrassed. In fact, she had looked forward to it, had asked him on more than one occasion if they could go to the baths twice a week. Likewise, he had taken great pleasure in scrubbing her body, lathering her small and undeveloped breasts with a smooth, flat stone he'd found on the banks of the Yellow River.

Now, it didn't matter where he went. He didn't mind the cigarette butts floating in Nun Min's pools, or the smell of feces migrating over from the bathroom next door. He scrubbed his body with efficiency, lathered in a way that allowed him to leave the water as soon as possible. He still kept the stone he'd use to wash Lin's body. It was locked away in a chest in his room, with the hope that it would one day be used again after the two of them had wed.

"How are you, Old Fu?" The man talking was Old Peng, a chubby cabbage farmer who had been wealthy until a section of his land was destroyed by a flood. He dipped his towel into the water, washed it, and then repeatedly slapped his shoulders until it stuck. "Getting yourself clean for the Spring Festival?"

Fu shook his head. He was in no mood for talk. Whenever he opened his mouth in a public bath, he thought about Lin and all the times they'd had together.

"What's keeping you down, old man?" Peng took a seat beside Fu. They had been close friends during their youth, though they didn't talk to each other often anymore. At their graduation ceremony, Peng had predicted, with accuracy, the woman his friend ended up marrying.

"It's Lin," Fu said. "I can't control her anymore."

Peng laughed. "Why don't you just marry her?" he said, as if the answer was simple. "Isn't that why you've been taking care of her?"

"How do you know what I'm thinking?"

"The entire village knows. We've seen the way you look at her out in the fields. I can't speak for everyone, but I think we've known about it for years, ever since you started taking her to the baths. Why else would you not find another wife? Why else would you take care of someone who's not your flesh and blood, and a *girl*, too?"

Fu was excited to hear Peng's words, but again he slumped his shoulders and shook his head. "It's no use," he said. "She won't have me as a husband."

"It doesn't matter what she will or will not have. All that matters is what you deserve. You've given her a home when no one else would, brought her up to be a fine young lady—maybe a little spoiled—but fine all the same. Old Fu, you are her savior, and she should be filial. Perhaps filial is the wrong word, but she should still be loyal. Think about it, Fu, you're also the only person *she* has. It's not too late to acquire a healthy son from the womb you've helped to nurture."

"You're right," Fu said. Renewed by Peng's words, he stood up and stepped out of the water. Embarrassed by his erection, he lowered his towel and tied it around his waist.

Peng shook with laughter. "Yes," he said. "It's definitely not too late, Old Fu."

Mr. Nan set the bottle of rice wine on the table. It was an expensive brand—Mao Tai—costing him a week's wage. He had not planned on visiting the family-planning commissioner. But Lin had insisted. She had told him that there was so much they didn't know about America—the cost of living, of marriage—that it'd be smart to have as many things settled as possible, marriage being the most important—and costly. The rice wine had also been her idea.

"So you say you want to marry Old Fu's daughter, Lin Song." The commissioner reached for the bottle and examined its label. "This is a delicate matter, Mr. Nan."

Nan's face changed to one of confusion. "How so?"

"As you may know, Miss Lin Song has not been always a village girl. She once lived in America, and every action needs to be taken with the utmost consideration and care."

"But surely there shouldn't be any objections when two people are in love. We have consented to being married."

The commissioner paid no attention. "Furthermore, another man is also interested in making Lin Hong his bride. You see, for me, Miss Hong's future is not so clear."

Nan grew concerned, scratching the spots on his neck. Had Lin been promised to another? Was she playing him for a fool?

"But don't look so glum, Mr. Nan. It's fortunate for you that the family-planning committee just had its monthly meeting two days ago. This will give me another month to think over the matter. In the meantime—"

"Has Lin consented to marry this other man?"

The commissioner smiled, showing a row of artificial white teeth. "That's something I can't tell you. As I was saying, in the meantime, write up a report to prove your mutual love. Depending on the report and other evidence"—he tapped on the bottle of wine—"I might be able to sway the committee to make a decision in your favor."

Nan got up. He wanted to take the bottle of wine back, feeling cheated that he'd spent so much money on a prospect that was now not such a sure thing.

After Mr. Nan had left, the commissioner stashed the wine in a cabinet behind his desk. The cabinet was lined with other bottles of expensive wine, and at the beginning of every month, he sold them at discounted prices to high-class restaurants and hotels. Having done this for twenty years, the commissioner had made many connections, including the owner of an underground mahjong ring, whose son was soon going to America, the commissioner's daughter being his bride. Now more than ever, they needed money—plane tickets, luggage, cell phones—forcing the commissioner to step up his operations. He had never wanted to give peasants a hard time, had always given his regards when they asked for marriage licenses, had even waived fees when peasant women gave birth to multiple children. But things had changed. Now, he needed to squeeze more money for his daughter. Examining Fu's papers side by side with Nan's, he wondered how much he could make from these men who were both so infatuated with this strange and out-of-place girl.

A few days later, Fu showed up to his office again, setting on his table a bottle of rice wine and a handwritten letter in support of his proposal. In it, he talked about the years he had spent as a widower and the deep love he had accumulated for Lin. He also pointed out the signatures of ten well-respected villagers, including Peng, who all agreed that he and Lin should wed.

"This is all very convincing," the commissioner said. "And I would like very much to approve your wedding, but you have to also be aware that another man had come asking for Lin's hand, and it would take more than sweet words to convince the other committee members of your devotion."

"I understand," Fu said, leaning in. "This other man, how enthusiastic was he when he came to you?"

"He was not very enthusiastic after he learned that another wanted to marry Lin. In all honesty, the committee is in your favor. Just give me fifteen hundred to two thousand *yuan*—of course, the more the better—and it'll make my life a lot easier when the committee meets."

More so than anxiety over the money, Fu felt relief. As soon as he got home, he began to make preparations.

Lin didn't know what Fu was up to these days. He was acting strange, even for him. The chicken coop was missing half its chickens, and the old bull was killed and sold to the butchers. Then one day, she noticed that the Qing-dynasty coatrack was also gone. When she asked what happened to it, Fu told her that he had sold it—in order to pay for Spring Festival festivities. She grew suspicious because Fu had never taken holidays seriously before. She watched him with narrowed eyes as he lugged away his silk beddings and expensive souvenirs. His *dayang* coins, a relic given to him by his grandfather, were pawned to Old Wisdom's Antique Shop.

"What are you up to?" she asked him again. They were eating chicken-cabbage soup. Fu drizzled the broth over his rice and scooped it up in sticky chopstickfuls.

"I told you. We're preparing for the Spring Festival."

"I don't see any new decorations, and we're eating worse than before."

"You'll see," he said. "When the Spring Festival comes, I have a surprise for you."

Lin kept silent. In the distance, she heard the school dance team practice the lion dance, mini-gongs crashing, opera singers belching to the accompaniment of string pianos.

"How's your situation with your science teacher?" Fu asked, looking up from his rice bowl. "Has Mr. Nan made any commitments yet?"

Lin picked up her chopsticks and started to eat. "He's grown a little distant," she said. "But he will marry me, make no mistake about that."

"It's best not to get one's hopes up," Fu said.

She ignored him. Mr. Nan had told her that they were a perfect match. Not only did they love each other, but he didn't need to worry as much about immigration since she had already been to

America. They had kissed while walking on the frozen pond, and when she tried to skate with her boots and fell, he had picked her up in the way that a husband should. She even grew accustomed to his scars, training her eyes to view them as beauty marks instead of deformities. If he *was* starting to lose interest in her, it meant only that she needed to renew his passion.

That night, she stayed up late, watching the American channel on CC-TV. She saw a man wearing a lab coat injecting a blue liquid into a test tube, and she imagined that he was Nan. She saw a couple running on a beach, their slippers flopping in white sand. She saw a neighborhood of identical two-story houses with a car parked in front. She saw all of these things, and it made her belly tingle knowing that she'd soon be a part of this world, that she'd soon be home again.

The first firecrackers were lit before dawn. Children lined the streets wearing red, bulgy cotton-stuffed coats and holding sticks attached to dragonfly and turtle kites. The lion dance, performed by the senior high school students, paraded through the village at first dawn, the ribbons of their silk costumes shimmering under the red morning sun. A percussion ensemble followed, the performers mostly old men, dancers themselves during their prime. Then there were trays filled with lotus cakes and berry-stuffed dumplings, the women who carried them doing their best to give each child only one.

Though everybody agreed that they'd rather live in the city for most days of the year, it was also common knowledge that, during the holidays, everyone wanted to be back in the countryside. High officials parked their cars in fallowing fields. The mayor brought his wife and grandchildren, wearing an army outfit adorned with medals. Even the family-planning commissioner came. When he reached Fu's house, he saw the old man waiting for him at the door, his arms behind his hunched back, smiling.

"Is it official?" Fu asked.

"Yes." The commissioner took out an envelope from a plastic bag. "But I wonder, Fu. How did you acquire so much money?"

"Never mind that," Fu said, his eyes on the envelope. "Is that it?"

"Yes. This is your marriage certificate. You only need Lin to sign it for it to become official."

Fu beamed. He took out the certificate and held it in the palm of his hands as if it were a divine order from Buddha. He looked across the field and saw Lin on the hill where the old well was. She was dressed in a red mandarin-collared blouse with slits on the sleeves. She carried a green silk handkerchief that she waved whenever she laughed.

"I take it that must be Lin," the commissioner said.

Fu nodded, folding the envelope in half and putting it in his pocket.

"I'll see you at the festivities, old friend." The commissioner walked through Fu's fields, up the hill where the villagers gathered, where they had a full view of the village as the band and dancers paraded around. He nodded when he saw Lin and bowed to the mayor who was standing in the middle discussing crop yields with the farmers. He turned and glanced at Lin again, who was laughing. He shook his head—if she were his niece or granddaughter or even his mistress—his emotion would be something similar to compassion.

Lin wasn't laughing due to happiness. She laughed because Nan was looking at her and holding her friend Yan's hand. Though she and Nan had grown distant over the last week, Lin had every confidence that he would still be hers. Naturally, for a man like him, he would want to test the waters before making a final decision. Lin understood. She also understood that she was better than Yan in every way: in beauty, in intelligence, in breeding, in the way she held herself. He'd soon grow bored of Yan and come back to her apologetically. If, for some reason, he still liked Yan after a few days, she would seduce him, sleep with him if she needed to. All the cards were in her favor. She just needed to wait until the time was right to act.

By midafternoon, about half the men were drunk. Fu summoned enough courage to walk up the hill and join the others. Perhaps he could try and find the right moment to talk with Lin. He had never liked holidays, had never liked being in a crowd. After his wife had died, he had felt embarrassed being a part of the mass funeral. He didn't like it when his feelings were lumped together with others. He tried to picture Lin's reaction when he asked her. He did not expect her to agree immediately, would be surprised, in fact, if she did. But he had the upper hand now. He would explain to her how perfect the match was, how well things would work out in the end. He had anticipated an answer to all her complaints, and he was certain she could not refuse him after she'd heard his case. After all, he was still her father in power, *entrusted* by her parents to make the right decisions for her.

When the sun began to set, the students stopped parading and put on their dragon sparring costumes. It was the show everyone was waiting for. Two dragons—one green, one red—each manned by twelve students, would spiral around the village in fierce combat. The green one represented earth, the red one heaven. Loud clashes of the gong signaled that the battle was about to start. The dragons first flew parallel to each other, then twisted and intertwined. Young boys followed dangling strings of firecrackers, the loud machine-gun pops displacing cardboard kernels onto the ground.

A twenty-seven-inch TV was brought up the hill and placed on the covered well. The sky turned violet; the village lanterns glowed underneath like a circle of ancestral spirits. It was custom for everyone in the village to watch the annual Spring Festival show, televised from Beijing.

The villagers stood up for the anthem. Even the costumed students, throwing the dragons on the ground, placed their hands over their hearts. The firecrackers were silenced. Everyone gathered around the well and watched the twenty-seven-inch TV as the Red flag rose. "Forward, forward, forward," the TV sang. The villagers loved this new China for providing them with so much stability. They thanked it for giving them the selfishness to take control of their lives.

FURTHER NEWS OF DEFEAT

A runner arrived at Xinchun Village two days after the fall of Taiyuan. Out of breath, his Kuomintang uniform soaked in sweat, the soldier collapsed into a fly-infested ditch on the edge of a sorghum field. That evening, San saw him on her way back from tending to her family's two goats, the man lying there snoring, and when she told her parents about him, they didn't believe her. San, nine years old, often lied to her parents. The Japanese were here one week, the Russians the next. Her parents knew San hated shepherding and dismissed her pleas to save the young man from becoming pig fodder. After putting her to bed, San's father slung a hoe over his shoulder and walked across his fields under moonlight to the place his daughter had mentioned. He couldn't lift the man out of the mud by himself, even after taking off his own shoes and using his bare feet for traction. He ran to the village chief, who sent a neighbor to help him. Together, with one man lifting the head and another the legs, they carried him to the granary and dropped him beside sacks of harvested sorghum.

The man remained unconscious the entire time. The villagers, observing the soldier clearly in the light, saw that he was only a boy: a scrawny, malnourished teen in a faded uniform and an oversized cap.

"I can't believe how heavy that kid was," BuDan said, wiping muddy sweat from his brow. BuDan's family farmed the land to the very west of Xinchun and he was his parents' only son. The strongest man in the village, he was often called upon to perform tasks that others couldn't: push a stubborn mule, transport tub-sized jugs of rice wine, carry replacement limestones for those worn away at the ancestral shrine.

"The mud weighed him down," said the village chief. He pointed to the canisters that rattled on the boy's belt. "We should've undressed him first."

BuDan slapped the boy a few times, and still, he would not wake. The village herbalist was called in and only after inserting slices of ginger into his nose did the boy finally start to shudder. He coughed out thick, brown water. San's father brought a bowl of rice porridge up to the boy's mouth, and the boy extended his thin neck to drink it.

After thanking the villagers squatting in the darkness in front of him, he broke into tears. "It's over," he said. "The Japanese flooded the Yellow River. Taiyuan was sacked."

The villagers glanced at each other. "What do you want us to do?" the village chief asked.

"I don't know," the boy said. He wiped his nose with his sleeve and sank his head below his shoulders. "My lieutenant never tells me anything. I think the Chinese army wants you to stay where you are."

"That's a strange message," San's father said.

"Useless," BuDan added, running his fingers through his hair. "So, we shouldn't flee?"

The chief told the two men to calm down. He gave the boy another gulp of water. "What would they do to us?" he asked. Rumors of Nanking had already reached the village. A hundred thousand dead in the span of six weeks. Men rounded up and gathered on the shores of the Yangtze, shot and burned and used for bayonet practice.

"I don't know," the soldier said. "They might not kill anyone outside the cities. How else are they going to get food?"

The villagers helped the boy up to his feet and filled a pouch with leek cakes and water and slung it over his shoulder. "Why don't you stay until morning?" the chief offered.

The boy shook his head. "I'm not tired anymore, and there are others who don't know."

Under the cover of night, they saw him off.

"Come back if you hear more news!" BuDan shouted.

San awoke excited the next morning. She put on her moss-colored coat and ran barefoot across the field to the fly-infested ditch near where her parents were gathering sorghum. Her father took off his straw hat, squinted at the sun, red as a morning rooster, and yelled for San to fetch him water.

"Where is my soldier?" San yelled back.

"He's gone!"

"What a shame," San whispered, looking down at the muddy ditch, which still traced the outline of the collapsed body. She had always wanted to be friends with a soldier.

They arrived four days later. One truck, one jeep. The villagers gathered in the town square: two brick-and-stucco buildings on sloped dirt ground, one used for a granary and the other for town meetings. The soldiers in the jeep got out first. The officer wore a brown suit with a black strap across his chest. He had a thin mustache and rested his gloved hand on the hilt of a sheathed saber. The other soldier, who had driven the jeep, ran around and unhooked the back latch of the truck, from which twenty soldiers came streaming out. Two of them carried a long pole. They attached a Japanese flag to one end, then stuck the other in the dirt. The rest of the soldiers formed a perimeter around San and her family and the villagers, blocking them from reaching the officer.

"You." The officer pointed at Lu Han, a carrot and cabbage farmer who lived adjacent to San and her family. "Begin the count."

The officer had a heavy accent and Lu mistook his meaning. He began to count—*yi, er, san, si*—and a soldier hit him with the butt of his rifle. The officer pointed in quick succession to each villager in the front row. "Begin again," he said, and the villagers counted off—*yi, er, san, si*—until everyone had a number. "From now on, you are known by your number. Every morning at seven, you will stand in the position you are in now and we will do the count. If someone is missing, the people whose number come before and after will be shot."

BuDan stood near the front of the line. His number was fourteen, and he made sure to shout it loudly and clearly. His family had the most to lose if he angered the Japanese. Not only did they own the most *mu* of land amongst all the villagers, BuDan was also quick-tempered. He enjoyed drinking wine and often doused himself after a hot day in the fields. As an only son, he understood that if something happened to him, his family would never survive a season.

San daydreamed during the count. When her number came—seventy-eight—her father counted for her. She was thinking about the soldier she had seen in the ditch, imagining him fighting these

Japanese all by himself. She picked at the moss-colored coat her mother had made for her during the Spring Festival. It had once had two life-sized mandarin ducks embroidered on each side, though her mother was clumsy with a needle and the silk thread began unraveling a week after San had started to wear it. Now, half a year later, only one duck remained, and already it was losing its webbed feet. San tugged off another loose thread and smoothed her coat.

Brushing a strand of hair away from her face, she thought the soldier standing in front of her looked ridiculous. His face was smeared with mud and he wore a strange gray hat that made him look like a bunny. She was standing beneath him, her father's hand stroking her hair, and she could smell the soldier's boots, the scent of polish. The soldier smiled at the pigtailed girl staring up at him, then gave her a wink.

The officer drove off in his jeep that same afternoon but one of his lieutenants remained with ten men. They brought in a table to the meetinghouse and set up a radio. Two soldiers guarded the entrance to the granary. When the villagers deposited wheat and sorghum, the soldiers put their nose to each bag. BuDan, sickened by the noise of the soldiers' high-pitched salutes and their radio static every time he made a deposit, hid half of his harvest in his outhouse.

Each morning after count, San sat on the ground with her back against the Japanese flagpole, petting her goats and watching the soldiers march from one building to the other. They didn't seem so bad. Some even helped older villagers carry bags of sorghum into the granary. She picked out the soldier who'd winked and gave him a name, Pointy, because the earflaps of his hat extended sharply up to his forehead, as if he'd cut them with a pair of scissors.

One morning, Pointy was moving a bag of wheat from the granary to the townhouse and tripped on some goat droppings wet from rain. San couldn't stop laughing—so loud the entire village might have heard. Even the lieutenant sitting inside came out and put on his glasses for a closer look. Pointy dusted himself off. His lieutenant nodded towards the girl, saying something in Japanese. San was still laughing when Pointy was standing in front of her. He unslung his rifle and stomped the butt end into the ground. Dust kicked up from his boots. San rose with a start. She rubbed her nose with her hand to avoid coughing. The soldier stared at her, his earflaps blowing in the wind. San saw that he had more lines on his forehead than even some of the older villagers. She couldn't tell how many of the lines were wrinkles or scars and couldn't guess his age. After a moment, the soldier turned around and slung his rifle back on his shoulder.

"You don't scare me!" San shouted.

Pointy stopped, slowly pivoting his head towards the girl. All of a sudden he charged at her with his rifle forward. In terror, she ran full bore all the way back to her house, through tall wheat stalks and muddy leek fields.

Her father was furious. "Where are the goats?" he yelled.

Her mother clutched San, who was crying, and yelled at her husband, "Forget your goats! Your daughter is frightened!" She sat on the furnace, cradling San in her lap. "What did those men do to you?" she whispered.

"My goats better not be in the hands of the Japs! Tomorrow morning if I smell goat stew coming from the townhouse—"

"Yell louder, so the whole town can hear," she said. Then she turned to San. "Look at your coat. Your duck looks so lonely and sick! When the Japanese are gone, we'll go to the city, and I'll buy another spool of silk and fix him up."

That night, San dreamed about Pointy. She saw him coming

at her with the rifle, this time with a bayonet attached. He drew closer and closer until suddenly his bayonet was buried inside her goat, and he was cutting off the goat's leg and carrying it back to the townhouse, where a huge cauldron with ladles sat on a stove, and everyone in the village was gathering for goat stew except her.

Early next morning, before the sun had risen, BuDan brought one of the goats back to San's family. The animals belonged to BuDan almost as much as they belonged to San's father. BuDan's ram had sired them and the two families had agreed, when the time came, to share the meat and have a banquet.

He knocked on San's father's door, and when it opened, told him that he had been passing by the town square yesterday, carrying a sack of grains, when he saw a soldier holding the leashes to their goats. He had argued with the soldiers, but they only gave him back the one.

"They killed the other this morning," he said. "I'm taking care of this last one myself. You have a coward for a daughter."

San's father took a sip of his tea and then spat out the leaves. "We should feel lucky they aren't roasting *her*."

Furious, BuDan kicked over a bucket of coals before leaving. San's father stepped back inside and fetched his wife and daughter for morning count.

At the town square, the villagers were surprised to see that the officer was back. A dozen soldiers stood by the jeep and truck. Both vehicles kept their engines running, and the two lead soldiers blew their bugles to quiet the crowds.

"Today is a glorious day for this village," the officer said. As he talked, the villagers counted off. They had been doing this for over a week now, barking their numbers and turning to the next person in swift, militaristic motions. "Today," the officer continued, "the Imperial Japanese Army will be taking volunteers to serve in its prosperous coal mine. You will be given food, uniforms, and a chance the Kuomintang never gave you: a chance to leave this village. You will have worker status and a new life under a new government. Please raise your hand, as spots are limited."

"What is he saying?" San whispered to her mother.

Her mother paid her no attention. They stood in the back, and San tried to peer through people's legs, but she couldn't see her soldier or hear the bells of her goat. There was only the hum of the truck and jeep, and the thickly accented Chinese that she could barely comprehend.

Two soldiers brought out a table and chair and placed them in front of the officer. The officer set his saber on the table and then sat down. He took out a pen and used his left hand to keep the paper from floating away. The other man from his jeep—his second officer—came forward. "Volunteers!" he yelled. "Step up!"

Nobody moved. The stillness held only the sound of the wind. Dust kicked up and gathered around the officer. The villagers thought the Japanese looked silly, their officer sitting at the desk beside the flagpole on the bumpy, sloped ground. They thought if the wind blew any harder the desk would slide past the granary and down into the garlic patch. Some hid smirks. "Japanese dogs," Hairy Taiping whispered to the person next to him. Hairy was a known troublemaker and got his nickname for serving pigs feet without bothering to remove the hair. "How stupid do they think we are?" he added.

"If there are no volunteers," the officer said, "then we will have to conduct a draft." He nodded to his second officer. "Every tenth male."

The second officer counted in Japanese as the soldier in front of him grabbed men by the arm and pulled them forward. Husbands were separated from wives, sons from mothers. Some villagers tried to flee but behind them a crescent of bayonet-wielding soldiers waited. Hairy Taiping tried to run through the lines and was shot instantly. He was not respected in the village, but even the women who had never cared for him burst into tears as he lay on the ground clutching his stomach, his cries silenced by two bayonet blows to the skull. San's mother covered San's eyes and wheeled her around towards the officer. "Look up at the flag," she said. "Look up at the way it blows."

San was crying. "What did Taiping do?" she asked.

By this time, the second officer had reached San's family. The tenth male was her father. Just as a soldier was reaching to pull him out of the crowd, another soldier—Pointy—pushed San's father away. "Not this one," Pointy said. "I've seen him work. He's lazy." And so the eleventh was picked.

When the soldiers finished, they loaded a total of twenty-three men into the truck. The crescent of soldiers also climbed in. The officer stepped onto his jeep and the vehicles began their descent down the hill. A third of the villagers ran after them, their feet kicking up as much dirt as a herd of cattle.

When the town square began to clear and only a few families remained, San saw Pointy kneeling down, his hands motioning for her to come over. She hid behind her mother's leg. Pointy held up his index finger and kept it there in front of him as he backed up into the meetinghouse and brought out several pieces of candy wrapped in glittering yellow paper. San let go of her mother and ran to him. She took two pieces from his hand and unwrapped one. The candy was creamy and sweet: preserved squid in honey. Suddenly, two hands lifted her by the armpits. Pointy twisted her around so that she was facing him and hanging from his hands.

"Let go," San shouted. She bashed at him, her fists clenched. Pointy's breath smelled like mushrooms and his tortoise shell hands were cold and sweaty on her torso.

Her father ran over and took San from the soldier. Pointy took off his hat and grinned. San glanced back several times, one hand holding her father's and the other clutching the candy, at Pointy waving to her as she made her way back to her father's sorghum fields.

That same day, after Hairy Taiping was mortally wounded, BuDan had stormed toward the shooter, and was met with the butt of Pointy's rifle. Pointy dragged BuDan's unconscious body behind the granary into the garlic patch. It wasn't until later that night that BuDan, awakened to a full moon, a headache, and the smell of budding garlic, trudged back home and found his mother crying by the furnace: his father had been one of the men taken.

Over the next few days, San's fear of Pointy gradually abated. Taking her position by the flagpole after morning count, she continued to observe the soldiers. Her father wanted to pull her away, but her mother reminded him that if it weren't for his daughter's connection with the soldier, he'd be working in a coal mine. "They're not going to do anything to a little girl," she said. "What can it hurt?" Sometimes Pointy would bring her cookies from Japan—green tea-flavored shortbread that dissolved in her mouth. He would ask her to do little things—spin around five times, show him her belly button, or sing him a song—before giving her the treats. She didn't know why Pointy liked her so much. Maybe he missed his daughter back home. Maybe he had lots of sisters while growing up. Maybe he just thought she was pretty.

Whereas the adults harvested their crops under constant alarm,

San had almost forgotten about Hairy Taiping's death. Her parents never told her why he was murdered, and San assumed he had made fun of a soldier. Hairy had often given her a hard time when she had shepherded the goats. He called her "goat girl" and slapped them on the rear to make her chase after them.

One afternoon, about a week after the officer had taken away the twenty-three men, San heard screams coming from the meetinghouse. She knew at once that these were not Chinese screams. They were too high-pitched, too succinct. She ran to the granary and saw Pointy with two soldiers carrying one of their own on a stretcher made of bamboo and empty sorghum sacks. Pointy pushed her away with one hand. He was crying, which surprised San, since she had never thought Pointy—or any Japanese (or any man, for that matter)—capable of crying. He yelled something incomprehensible at her, and she ran home.

The Japanese dug a grave and buried the dead soldier behind the meetinghouse in the garlic patch where he had been found dead, his neck slit open. Then they fired off three shots in unison.

Two days later, the officer returned again to Xinchun, this time with two trucks. Soldiers created two perimeters, one surrounding the people at the town center and another loosely encircling the entire village. They wore backpacks and helmets, and it was clear that these soldiers were better trained than those that had come before them.

"I have been more than lenient," the officer began. Four soldiers had gotten out of the jeep. They stood in pairs, two behind the officer and two upfront, bayonets fixed. "And I will continue to be lenient, if someone will step forward and tell me who committed this crime."

The villagers were silent. Two soldiers brought out a large framed picture from the jeep and held it up for all to see.

"This is the man you killed," the officer continued. "Here he is with his family in Tokyo. His wife is pregnant with a girl, and this afternoon, I wrote to her that her husband will never see his daughter. Now"—he paused—"who killed this man?"

Silence. Half a mile away, the rapids of the Yellow River churned.

BuDan gave no indication that he was the one who had killed the Japanese soldier. *Why are they waving that picture?* he thought. Hairy Taiping had never been photographed in his life. Nor had his father or any of the other villagers who had been driven away to die in a coal mine. The soldier in the picture had shown no hesitation when he yanked those men from the lines and sent them off to work as slaves. Why should he be pitied?

BuDan had stalked him for two days. He watched him from the fields, taking note of his patrol route, observing when he rested and when he worked. Every time the soldier laughed with his friends, ate from his canteen, or saluted his superior, BuDan's hatred grew. At home, he told his mother what he would do to the soldier if given the opportunity. "Don't be a fool," his mother said. "Your father could still be alive. This is no time for vengeance." He accused his mother of not loving her husband, and on the following day, he waited until the soldier was by himself pushing a wheelbarrow loaded with a heavy sack of sorghum. BuDan approached, and the soldier dropped the wheelbarrow and lifted his rifle. Raising his arms, BuDan gestured that he only wanted to help the soldier with the sack. The soldier nodded. He was young, no older than twenty, and his end of the sack dragged as they carried it into the granary. "Heavy," the boy said in Chinese, embarrassed. BuDan closed the door and shoved him to the ground. He pressed the boy's face to the dirt, his palm flat over the boy's mouth and nose, took out a pocket knife, and slit the boy's throat.

"If no one is brave enough to step forward," the officer said, "then the man must have fled the village. You will all help us look for him."

The soldiers set the framed photograph of the boy on the table and instructed the villagers to gather in two long lines. Then they marched two sorghum fields away to the town's main well, where three dozen soldiers were already waiting at the top of the hill.

"We must prepare for the long search," the officer said. "We will first make sure no one gets thirsty."

Around the well there were ten buckets tied to levers, and the opening was so big that villagers often joked that they could push in an elephant. Moss covered the limestone bricks, displaying the stencils of children's handprints. During the fall and winter, the well was used as a means of preserving meat and steamed buns. A couple of families shared a single bucket and disputes often broke out as to whose food belonged to whom.

The two lines of villagers stopped at the entrance to the well. For every five or six people, a soldier stood on either side of the lines. San and her father were in one line and her mother was in the other. They were about a third of the way up the hill. "What's happening?" San asked. "We're getting water," her father said.

BuDan stood towards the back of the line. He first suspected that something was wrong when he heard the hollow echo of buckets crashing down into the water at the bottom of the well. The lines started moving, and then he heard screams. "They're stabbing us with bayonets and throwing us into the well!" someone shouted. The lines were moving fast. In front of BuDan, villagers were running away and getting shot. He turned to the nearest soldier, grabbed him by the arm, and kneeled before him. "I'm the one you want," he said. "Tell them you've found me. I killed your friend." But the soldier shoved him aside and BuDan realized that he didn't understand what was saying. The soldier must've thought he was begging for his life. BuDan held his arms over his head, surrendering. "I'm the one you want!" he shouted, but nobody, neither the villagers nor the Japanese, seemed to be hearing him.

San watched her mother being dragged away to the opening of the well. A soldier stabbed her twice, then lifted her legs and threw her in. Another soldier did the same to San's father. San tried running away but a hand caught her elbow. When she looked up, she saw that it was Pointy. He pulled her to the opening of the well, and for a second she stood there shivering, waiting for him to stab her. "Jump!" Pointy said. "Jump before someone kills you!" San couldn't understand him through his accent, and when she didn't move, he lifted her up. She felt his facial hair jagged against her scalp, and then he was moving away from her, her vision closing off into a circle, becoming smaller and smaller until she hit the piled-up bodies at the bottom. A string of something hard and jagged—knuckles, perhaps—nicked her spine.

The well's walls were damp and jagged, lined with sharp stones. She was lucky not to have hit the sides. A thin beam of light shot down from the opening and half-illuminated the bodies. The well was almost a third full. The people who landed in first had drowned, and those lying in the middle were suffocating and bleeding. San stayed close to the wall to avoid the bodies that kept falling.

Below her came cries and groans. She listened for her parents, but all the voices sounded the same. Every few seconds there would be a scream, then a thump, and then another body would be next to her. Sometimes the man or woman was still alive when they landed.

She hugged her legs into her arms and looked at the one remaining mandarin duck on her coat. It was barely visible, but she could tell that it wasn't green anymore, that there was blood on it. She wondered if she was seeing all of this through the eyes of her own ghost. She wondered if she was also dead, like the other duck that had once been on her coat before she pulled it off slowly, month after month. Why had she done that? Why couldn't she have resisted the urge to tug at the thread and just let it be?

After a while, the bodies stopped falling and the well grew silent. They reached all the way up to the opening. San waited until the sun began to set and the voices of the soldiers had grown distant. Then she started climbing. She didn't know where she would go after she got out. She had never been outside of the village before. She thought of Pointy, of how he had saved her life. If she hurried, she might be able to find him.

It was becoming difficult to see. The opening was orange-red, the color of the setting sun. Sometimes she would grab onto an arm and it would slip, sending her several bodies down. She grappled for a hand, a foot, or—if she could—a head; she found that her small hands held onto hair the best. When she was at the top, she reached for a rope tied to a bucket and brought her legs over the stone ledge.

A full moon was beginning to rise. She heard the distant rumble of trucks and started running in that direction. Tired from the climb, she collapsed near the town entrance and fell asleep in a patch of wheat.

The day after the massacre, though he had heard no news of it, the runner returned to Xinchun. He was not initially surprised when he didn't see anyone in the streets or out in the fields. He had heard about the coal mine, and suspected that the entire village might have been transported there. In some ways he felt relieved. He was able to go from house to house and search for food and supplies without asking anyone.

He went to the granary and found the entire stock of sorghum empty. "What a shame," he said. He gathered old pears and scattered cloves of garlic and made his way from the west of the village to the east.

He was walking up to the well to refill his canteen when he noticed the smell. Flies as thick as falling rain hovered around the opening. Halfway up the hill, he saw an arm falling over the ledge. He didn't need to walk any farther. He turned around and began eating a pear, trying to divert his nose from the smell of the rotting corpses.

Upon reaching the town's entrance, he saw a girl lying in a wheat field. She wore a faded green coat made from imitation silk—peasant fabric. Reaching a hand over to see if she was still alive, he saw the subtle rise and fall of her body, hidden before by the rustling wheat. He knelt down and took her pulse: as quick as a hopping rabbit. He thought about waking her up, but then he thought about the twenty-mile walk back to his division's camp. He backed away. Having had his rest, he took off in a light jog, making his way out of the valley and then up the mountain, back to his lieutenant to deliver this further news of defeat.

THE WELL

For over three hundred years, since the return of the two brothers
Ai and Jiu, our family has been known across the province for our
ability to dig and construct wells. According to our ancestral tree,
the two brothers joined Li Zicheng's coalition of rebel forces against
the Ming Dynasty and partook in the 1644 sacking of Beijing. When
the Qing army came and destroyed Li Zicheng's army, they returned
home to Xinchun and lived a pastoral life of farming and well drilling. The brothers were large and fearsome, built like upright mules,
and when I was little, I often went to the shrine of my ancestors to
stare at the limestone engravings of their silhouettes, at their hair
tied in dense buns, at their beards, long and flowing, that made
them look like warrior-poets, and at their eyes, generous and determined, that embodied a confidence and spirit that nowadays villagers and city folk alike seem to lack.

For example, just the other day, my wife, Tingting, and I drove our tractor to Yuncheng City to sell off our excess peppers. We were setting up shop along Golden Destiny Lane, a popular tourist spot, grinding our dried peppers into chili for people to sample, when a tour guide—one of those jobless local men who owned a three-wheeled taxi—got out of his vehicle and helped the rich tourist get up from his seat. The guide, skinny with shrunken cheeks, might as well have gotten on his hands and knees and hailed the rich tourist as the next coming of Buddha. Even though he was taller, the guide kept his head hunched. The tourist carried a cane and walked over to taste our chili. After sampling a pinch on his tongue, he said, "Too hot," and then motioned for the guide to bring him something to drink. The guide handed him a glistening bottle of water, one in a plastic container that young people—my daughter included—seem to like, and the tourist drank half of it down in a hurry and then threw the bottle to the ground, where the water funneled out like blood from a headless chicken. He then had the nerve to tell the guide that the water was hot. And the guide, instead of spitting on the man's face, apologized! They didn't buy any of our chili, and I'm glad they didn't because I wouldn't have sold them any; not to the tourist, for being a wasteful slob, and not to the guide, for shaming the Chinese people.

Until recently, my family went to the city only when we needed to buy materials we couldn't get in the countryside. We didn't need to use our own hands to sell off our extra crops; we made enough money from our well-digging to hire other people. We are still the dominant well diggers in our region. From Xinchun to Duchun to Pingchun, we are occasionally called upon to dig new wells, but most of our work nowadays is to repair old ones. My daughter, Guo, tells me I should expand the family business by using modern equipment and by *drilling* on our property to bottle and sell water. I tell her drilling is disrespectful, unnatural, and bad for the soil. She tells me my beliefs are nonsense, superstition. I tell her that if it weren't for this "superstition" passed down by our ancestors, I would've never had enough money to send her to agricultural college, where she learned those fancy drilling techniques.

"Oh, Dad," she says, "if you wear a glove for too long, you risk outgrowing it."

"I'm old," I tell her. "My hands stopped growing long before you were born."

There has been a drought of work over the last few months. My family is getting short on spending money (we've already sold most of our extra chili). Then, one day, Boiled Dan, the village chief of Duchun, taps on my door carrying cartons of haw flakes and Coca-Cola. I know what he wants from the moment he steps into my yard, and I feel an excitement that I haven't felt since I was nine, when my father took me to dig my first well.

"Jiang!" he says, handing my wife the cartons tied together with bright orange ribbons. "Is it true what they say about the Lao's, that the older they get, the stronger their arms?"

Boiled Dan is not a man to be trusted. He treats you like an emperor when he needs something and turns his back like a feathered peacock after getting what he wants.

"Our arms strengthen with our sons," I say, nodding to Tingting. "This one is barren of teakettle chutes."

Tingting places the cartons in a cabinet next to the stove. She has heard my complaint ten thousand times—it's almost a joke between us—and automatically she says, "One cannot be blamed if the original teakettle leaks."

"Quick-witted as always, Tingting." Boiled Dan smiles and I see a shining silver tooth in between yellowed ones. "But let me do away with formalities. I have come to ask your family, the famous Lao well-diggers, for a favor."

I sit down, cross my legs, and ask him to continue.

He takes a seat across from mine and pours himself some tea. "As you may know, two weeks from now is Duchun's thirty-fifth anniversary. That's right: It's been thirty-five years since Chairman Mao came to our land and partitioned the gentry's property. I want to celebrate. I think we *should* celebrate. I want to give my villagers a new well, one as large and as grand as the largest in Xinchun."

I reach for the cigarettes in my shirt pocket. I insert one into my plastic holster and light it with a match. Puffing on it, I put on an expression of concern. "This is not a small order, Dan. Our well was built a long time ago, and I'm not sure if we still have the techniques to construct one of that size."

"But surely well-building flows from you like sweat. Surely this is a job meant for villagers. Surely having you is better than hiring private contractors from the city." And here is the real reason he comes to me: to save him money. He smiles, his eyes disappearing. He knows I'll be flattered even if the flattery is so obvious.

I run my hand on the stubble of my beard. "I have to talk with the crew."

"Of course," he says, getting up to leave. "Remember, though, we don't have much time. I want to unveil it in two weeks, in time for the anniversary, and the sooner you decide to do it, the sooner your crew can start."

The next day, I decide to go up the hill with Tingting and my daughter to take measurements of Xinchun's central well. Our central well is one of the oldest and largest in the entire province. I know because my family must have constructed at least half of them. When I was young, my father and I would go from village to village taking surveys, making sure the village chiefs still had our address in case they needed repairs. On these trips, my father read me poetry by Li Bai and made me learn the classics: *Hong Lo Meng, Shui Hu, Journey to the West.* I was more interested in working with my hands, in well-digging, but I'm thankful that my father stressed the importance of literature. I'm known now in Xinchun as somewhat of a scholar. Occasionally, the village chief would come to me for help in deciphering a new code or ordinance, and this has brought a lot of respect for my family, and I like to think that my wife and daughter are proud of my knowledge.

But today, Guo is in a sour mood. She's mad at me because I didn't tell her fiancé, Fai, about Boiled Dan's proposition. It's not that I don't like Fai—I like him a lot; in fact, Tingting and I were the ones who arranged the wedding—but Fai is weak for a man, easily bullied by my daughter. Tingting and I thought this was good at first. Guo has such a strong personality, and we figured Fai's water might douse her fire. But recently I'm starting to regret my decision to marry my daughter to Fai, who is now second-in-command of the crew, a man I'm supposed to groom so that he can take my place and carry on the Lao family name. I'm afraid he will give in to my daughter's insistence. I'm afraid he's not going to uphold the traditional methods.

The three of us are silent on our way up the hill, but once we've reached the top, my daughter can't control herself anymore. "He'll see, you know," Guo says. "He will see us by the well and suspect we're hiding something from him. *Him*, my future husband. What am I going to say when he pressures me?"

"You'll tell him the truth, that as of now, I haven't agreed to anything. Besides, we both know Fai cannot pressure a hen to lay an egg."

"Stop lying to yourself, Dad. We all know you're going to take the job."

I pretend not to hear her. I crouch down next to the well, take out my tape measure, and hand it to Tingting. "Stay," I say, and then I begin to circle the opening. Cold air rises from the depth of the well, and with it, I smell an aroma of steamed buns and leeks. It's only September, and the well isn't quite chilled enough, but already villagers are using it as a refrigerator.

"Your daughter is right," Tingting says. "Soon Fai must be the one to start making decisions like this."

"What do you know? A wife wishing an early death on her husband will be scorned by Buddha for all her lives to come."

Tingting drops the tape measure. It coils halfway around before I let go of my end.

My daughter picks it up and hands it to me. "You know what she meant, Dad. The world is changing. A lot of villages use running water now. Soon, if you don't let us young people help you, there won't be many more decisions to make."

"Fine," I say, waving them away. "Go and get Fai. We need another man here. The two of you are more trouble than you're worth."

Fai and I spend the entire day gathering information. He is smart, possessing a scientific mind. Whereas I remember measurements by memory, he takes notes on a sheet of grid paper. His family was too poor to send him to college, but he was one of Xinchun's top students, on par with Guo. He knows his multiplication tables and how to use a calculator, and his back has grown strong from working in his family's fields.

After taking measurements of the well's circumference, width, its height above land, and the size of each of its bricks, we decide it's time to go down and measure its depth. We pull up a bucket and empty the steamed buns inside. Fai takes out a flashlight from his toolbox and hands it to me. Because he is the stronger of the two, I am the one who'll be lowered down. I step one foot into the bucket, grasp my right hand tight around the pulley, and hold the flashlight with my other hand.

It's been about fifty years since anyone has gone down. My ancestors used the finest marble brick mix to ensure the well's longevity. It's the reason the well hasn't needed any major restorations for over a hundred and fifty years. In fact, the last time someone went down was during World War II, when the Japanese used the well as a living grave, throwing in over half of Xinchun's villagers. The Red Road Army arrived a month after the massacre, and at first they thought the entire village was decimated, but people had hid in huts and fields and my young grandfather had gone to a neighboring village. Mao's soldiers tied shirts over their faces when they went down, and it took the Red Road Army two weeks to pull up all the bodies. Three years after the war, my father said the water was still tinged pink.

Shining the flashlight on the side of the well, I see that the walls could use some cleaning. The brickwork has become uneven in places, jagged, and it's likely that buckets might get stuck. The bricks are also covered with green moss. It's not poisonous, but the scent is damp and pungent, and the smell might migrate over to the buns and leeks. I'm surprised that over all these years I've gotten no complaints.

I count the number of bricks from the opening to the bottom, and when the bucket hits water, I shout, "Two hundred and ninety-nine," my voice echoing up. The pulley shifts a little. I step down into the water and it reaches my waist. Peering down at me, Fai looks no larger than an insect—an ant or grasshopper perched on heaven's doorstep. He disappears for a moment to tie the pulley to a rock or a tree, and I see him again with his clipboard of grid paper.

His mouth moves, and half a second later I hear his words echo down: "How large is the base?"

What makes this well such an interesting one is that the brick-work arches and becomes wider the deeper you go. At the bottom, the diameter has increased by at least a third. I submerge under-water, and to my surprise, there is a thin layer between the last brick and the earth, allowing the aquifer more room to move around, producing fresher water.

I count the number of bricks in the last circle and yell up, "Eigh-teen." The opening, if I remember correctly, has a circumference of twelve bricks.

Fai writes it down, tiny hands on tiny paper. I lift my foot into the bucket, pull my body up, and then tug at the pulley twice to let him know that I'm ready to be lifted back up. He disappears again. I'm sixty-seven years old, and to this day I rarely feel tired, even after a day of work in the fields, but right now, my arms are exhausted. Perhaps my tiredness is a trick of the mind. Perhaps finding out firsthand the intricacies of the well's design and the hours of labor required to reproduce it have gotten me scared. Whatever the rea-son, halfway from the top, I grow fearful that I might let go of the pulley and fall. I break one of the first rules of well repair: I look down, and I'm high enough so that I can't see the bottom. Even the glow of the flashlight does not reach the water, where only minutes ago my head was submerged.

"I don't think it's possible," Fai says, "at least without the use of modern equipment."

Guo sets a dish of pan-fried peanuts onto the table, smiles at me, then rejoins Tingting by the stove to cook the rest of the dinner.

"We can use equipment to make the bricks, of course," I say, "because of time constraints."

Fai looks over to my daughter for help. She gives him a nod, and he turns back to me. "Dad," he says, "what I mean is—"

"Elder Lao," I tell him. "No one is married yet."

"Elder Lao, what I mean is it'll save us a lot of money and labor to use a driller. Guo says she can borrow one from her college at no charge."

This is the first time Fai has been present in the early planning stages, and I forgive his words because he doesn't know the importance of tradition in well-digging. Since I'm supposed to be the one to teach him, this is partly my fault. "An apprentice," I say, "should not give the artisan advice. He should follow the artisan no matter what, like a son to a father. You will be both soon, so you should be doubly obedient."

Fai lowers his head. I hear the crash of a pot, and from the corner of my eye, I see Guo picking it up in such a manner as to let me know that she intentionally dropped it.

"Eat," I say, gesturing with my chopsticks. "This is no day to be glum. A project like this warrants celebration. Guo! Tingting! Bring out the wine!"

The next morning, a fog covers the roads. It is a portent for misfortune, and usually, with less pressing matters, I would've stayed home. I'm driving our tractor to Duchun, where Boiled Dan waits with the contract. Fai is sitting in the wagon with two of the crew. Guo also insisted that she should come, and since I'd won such a huge victory over her and Fai the day before, I decided to let her.

The tractor has both its advantages and disadvantages in foggy weather. It's slow enough that I won't crash into anything, but its speed also hinders it from making any sharp turns in case another vehicle fails to see us. Most of the time this isn't a problem, since the tractor is so loud that if the car doesn't see us, it should for sure hear us.

We arrive at Boiled Dan's house unharmed for the most part. Little Maize, a nineteen-year-old boy we hired two summers ago, had to jump off the tractor momentarily because his face was brushing against a tree branch, but luckily for us, no car was passing by at the time.

Boiled Dan's front door is open, and when we walk in, we see him in his yard sweeping eggshells into a pan. "Ah, Jiang," he says, "what took you so long?"

"The fog," I say.

"Right." He laughs. "I'm blind."

We are all amazed by the way his yard looks. I haven't been to his house in a few years, but I don't remember the whitewashed walls, the calendar of foreign cars, the large vase with dried cherry blossom branches sticking out, the brand-name electric stove, stainless steel pots, and bronze wok. "Stop staring," I tell the crew, but even Guo can't help walking over to the kitchen and admiring the cookware.

"Come in," Dan yells from the living room. "You don't have to stand outside. I've set out some treats."

The inside of his house is even more impressive than the courtyard: leather sofas, bamboo coffee table, and a thirty-two-inch TV, which is five inches larger than Xinchun's community TV. Fai and the others are already eating the moon cakes and sesame crisps that Boiled Dan set out on the table, and Dan pats the seat next to him on the sofa for me to sit down. The armrest feels cool on my elbow, like snakeskin, and I'm self-conscious when I lean back.

"I got some bad news, old friend." Dan has grown solemn. "I just got a call from Yuncheng this morning. The city contractors made me an offer I couldn't refuse."

"That can't be true," I say. "You gave me your word. We already drew up plans." I take out the well manifest from my back pocket and spread it out on the table. "You see here. We've chosen the techniques and materials. We're ready to begin work."

"Let me finish. Not all of my news is bad." He looks around at the crew, at Fai, at Little Maize, and then at my daughter. "The contractors are short on labor, and I recommended your crew. They faxed over a contract."

I shake my head. "Why hire more people when we could do it ourselves?"

"It's not a matter of people. It's time and cost. The village needs the well soon, and I can't take the risk of a delay. Plus, the contractors already have materials stockpiled, whereas we'd have to purchase our own at a premium price."

When he tells me this, I understand that this has been the plan all along. He never intended for us to work alone, to oversee the construction. In his eyes, we're just labor.

"We won't do it," I say. "You can look for slaves elsewhere, Dan."

"Why use such words, old friend? This is better for both of us. You might be getting paid less, but you'll be doing *much* less work, and money is still money."

Guo puts her hand on my shoulder, leaning in. "We do need money, Dad. Fai and I are getting married, remember?"

"What a sensible daughter you have," Dan says.

"Who told you to talk?" I say over my shoulder. "Go outside, all of you!"

The crew gets up from the couch. Guo takes Fai's hand into hers, and before she leaves the room, she says, "I have a wise, learned father. He reads poetry and understands it. I know he will see past his pride and make the right choice."

"Listen to your daughter," Dan says. "Here, as a show of good faith, I'll even add this." He places three one-hundred *yuan* bills onto the table. Then he takes out a contract written up by the city contractors and places it next to the bills. "So, old friend, how about it?"

After signing the contract, I walk outside with Boiled Dan. Everyone is relieved when they see the smile on Dan's face, the flash of his silver tooth. Guo hugs Fai, who, from the way he rubs his head, seems to be the most relieved of them all. He will soon be a husband, and after that, a father, and the only hope I have in the world now is for him to be luckier than me when it comes to his wife bearing him sons.

The crew has started to gather on the tractor, and I ask Dan if we can at least examine the location of the well.

"Of course," he says. "Just follow me." He walks around his yard to a shed in the back, where he brings out a black scooter covered in plastic wrap.

"Would you like a ride?" he asks.

I tell him no, that I need to drive the tractor.

"Well, what about you, Guo?" he says. "A beautiful young lady on a beautiful young vehicle."

She looks at me and I shake my head. "Sure!" she says, jumping on.

We drive behind Dan, following a dirt road, my daughter sitting behind him with her arms grasping the handlebars above the rear wheel. They're much faster than us, and every minute or two, they double back. The scooter kicks up dust, and combined with the fog, the road becomes difficult to see. I cough from the exhaust.

"Is that necessary?" I ask Dan when he doubles back again. "I can fit the two of you in the wagon. There's enough room for the scooter, too."

"Lighten up," Dan says, flashing his silver tooth. "Have a little fun."

"Yeah, Dad. Have a little fun." Guo winks.

When they disappear into the fog again, Fai taps me on the shoulder. "Is she safe? Should I do something?"

"You've missed your opportunity," I tell him. "You shouldn't have let her get on in the first place. Let this be a lesson."

We reach a bulldozed area of land on a small dirt hill, the fog preventing us from seeing where it begins to descend. Dan rides around the hill with ease, as if he was in his backyard, treading his scooter in concentric circles, twisting like a tornado. I grow increasingly worried for my daughter, who spins around so fast that I'm afraid she'll be thrown off. Boiled Dan holds his right hand into the air, as if touching the fog, and directs us to a spot on the ground marked with the red character *jing*—for well.

"Here," he says, and I'm somewhat astonished by the quality of the spot he picked. Of course, he has seen the location of Xinchun's well, and the bulldozed hill we're standing on reminds me a little *too* much of Xinchun's. Except our hill is natural. When the crew and I walk down, we see a pond nearby and a stream feeding into it. I'm impressed that Dan knows to place a well by a body of water—to track the aquifer level.

"Good choice of location," I tell him. "How do you know so much about well-digging?"

"The internet," he says. "My son just bought me a computer."

"You're not afraid of being electrocuted?" I ask. Wall outlets terrify me. When the Red Guards ran power lines through our village, my father was standing underneath one of the poles. The guards were not much more than kids and didn't know how to properly string up the wires. A couple of days later, the power was turned on, and the loose cable struck my father, killing him.

"Don't be silly, Jiang," Dan says. "The computer doesn't have enough power to harm a mouse." He gets on his scooter and puts on his blue Mao cap. "Jiang, I used to be like you, fearful of everything. But ever since I've embraced this New China, my life has gotten ten thousand times better." He takes out a cigarette, lights it with a golden lighter. "And I can still hold onto our traditions: why else would I build a well if I didn't value traditional village ways! You need to realize that the new and the old aren't mutually exclusive. You *can* have one with the other."

By the time we leave Boiled Dan's village, the fog has abated. Guo says she has to buy some sewing material from the city, and since Duchun is closer to Yuncheng than our village, we take a detour to visit Yuncheng's indoor market.

I've never been to this market before, but Tingting and Guo have gone several times since it opened four years ago. They tell me how convenient it is to shop here, how you push around this small metal cart and take whatever you want off the shelves and pay for all of it when you're done. "A thief's paradise!" I said, but walking around it now, I'm surprised that no one is stealing anything. Or maybe they're just such good thieves that I don't notice. Whatever the case, I'm not very impressed. I walk with my hands behind my back and tilt my head to examine the labels on the boxes and bottles. All of them say "Great Tasting" or "Delicious Flavor," but how do you know what is really good without someone there telling you what you're buying? Guo and Fai seem to know what they're buying, though, taking one item after another as if this was the way people had bought things throughout history. Even Little Maize, barely a man, finds a thing or two he likes.

I have been coming to Yuncheng for nearly fifty years now, first with my father, then with my wife, then with my young daughter, and now with my daughter and her soon-to-be husband. When I was a boy, Yuncheng seemed to me an old city. Its four-hundred-year-old walls were still standing. The fashionable men and women living here wore silk gowns that hid their ankles. And the older people had long flowing beards and haircuts like my ancestors—tied in dense buns. The streets were dirt or cobblestone, red candlelit lanterns hanging from every store, and there was a peaceful bustle about it all. Walking down its avenues, hearing the footsteps of the rickshaw man, smelling the roast duck hanging from restaurants, I felt like my grandmother was telling me a story.

Now, as an old man, Yuncheng seems to me a young city. The walls have long been dismantled—the Red Guards called them reminders of China's backwardness. Everybody on the streets has phones without wires, small enough to hold in your hands. And the older city folks dress in the same way that young people dress, in the same kinds of clothes, the women wearing the same kinds of makeup. You cannot cross the streets anymore without a car, a truck, or a bicycle hitting you, and everyone seems so busy, so important, even when they're just shopping for food.

I look up at the buildings and wonder where all of them came from. Some of the buildings must be as tall as our well is deep. They scare me when I walk by. I'm afraid they might fall.

CURES AND SUPERSTITIONS

I.

When the package of tiger bones and alligator tails arrived with the monthly shipment of fertilizer, Old Wisdom pasted a neon-green sign in front of his antique and herbal supply store with two words: THEY'RE HERE! His son, Ming, had bought the paper in Yuncheng City. He had typed up the characters on his computer, blowing up the font and making it blocky. Twenty years old, Ming despised working for his father, who never paid him so much as a *yuan*. Ming had done well in school, top 5 percent of his class, but only the top 2 percent got into college. His older brothers had their own families, his mother was dead, and his sister had married out of Xinchun Village to a doctor from Shanghai. Ming was the only one left to tend the fields, his arthritic father in no shape to do anything but package the herbal medicine and man the cash register. To Ming, a popular product like tiger bones simply meant additional labor.

Word of Old Wisdom's shipment traveled fast. By mid-afternoon, a line spiraled around the store's only aisle and out to the street's bicycle racks. Ming stood next to his father, weighing out grams of ground tiger bones and wrapping them in old editions of *The People's Daily*.

"Mix a pinch of this with a clove of strong ginseng," Old Wisdom told a young woman who was buying the tiger bones for her grandmother. "It won't cure her pain, but it will relieve it for several hours. If you need any ginseng, I have some right here." He motioned for his son to grab a box from the top shelf.

Ming threw the triangular box onto the glass tabletop.

After the woman left, Old Wisdom leaned in to his son, whispering, "You see: mention the other products, make two sales at once."

Ming hated being in the store. The individual products—snakeskin flakes, dried seaweed, and now tiger bones—didn't smell good to begin with, but their odors mixed to create a bitter, vomit-like stench. When he was five years old, he had gotten chickenpox, and his father had brewed him a black, tar-like stew. He hadn't asked his father what was in it, but he remembered it being the most disgusting thing he'd ever tasted, thick as sesame oil and twice as pungent as the bitterest bitter melon. Worst of all, the medicine didn't help; he was sick for over a month. Tigers were nearly extinct, and it saddened Ming to think that they'd died so uselessly.

Behind the counter and underneath the ginseng, Old Wisdom was brewing tiger bones with fig leaves in a kettle. He poured it into a ceramic cup, added jasmine tea, and, between customers, took sips.

"You want some?" he asked his son, who shook his head. "It's also great for *preventing* pain."

To meet demands, Old Wisdom kept the store open until eight, until the summer sun turned red and began to set behind the Blood Cloud Mountains. He was just about to lock the doors and turn off the lights when a car pulled up along the dirt road.

"You caught us just in time," he said, keeping the door open. Then he turned to Ming and shouted, "Don't take away the scale yet. We have another customer."

The man got out of the car—a gleaming black Mercedes—and slammed the door. He wore a striped tie and a dark blue suit left unbuttoned. Walking towards the store with the red sun behind him, he seemed to Old Wisdom like a messiah, like Buddha or Confucius if they had chosen to don modern attire.

Old Wisdom looked at his feet as the man entered. The man scanned the aisle, picking up boxes and then putting them back, on occasion lowering his sunglasses to read a label.

"You have a nice little store here," the man said. "A nice country store."

"Thank you," Old Wisdom said. "What are you looking for? Perhaps I can help."

The man approached the counter. "I'm here in your village to do business, but along the way, I thought I'd pick something up for my wife. She's pregnant, you see."

Old Wisdom grew solemn, nodding. "Might I suggest some tiger bones?" He pointed at the pouches on the counter. "It's very fresh; we just got this shipment in today. It's expensive, but I'm sure your wife is worth every penny."

Ming, who had been in the back of the store putting away product, entered carrying a pouch of alligator tails, ready to be separated and sold for tomorrow. It was rare for the store to have customers from the city, and he couldn't help but stare at the man and his nice clothes. The man seemed equally intrigued by Ming. He stared back at the boy with the intensity of a panther stalking its prey.

"Is this your son?" the man asked.

"Yes," Old Wisdom said. "This is my son, Ming."

"How old is he?"

"Twenty," said Old Wisdom.

The man reached into his breast pocket and took out a card. "Your son is exactly the type of person I'm looking for." He laid the card on the glass tabletop. "You see, I'm a labor scout. I look for young, strong men from the countryside and bring them to work in the city."

Ming walked over to the counter and picked up the card. On it, there was a name, Zhang Sha, and a position, Director of Search. At the bottom, there was a phone number. Ming didn't recognize the area code.

"I'm not supposed to tell anyone outside of the high school that I'm here, but as soon as I saw your son walk in, I knew he would be interested."

"I'm not sure," Old Wisdom said. "Ming has a bright future in the village."

"Well," said the man, "most likely he won't even beat the odds. With a village this size, there must be a hundred young men who want to leave. We're having an assembly tomorrow."

"What assembly?" Ming asked. "I've never heard of it."

"We like to keep it small. We don't want mobs forming." The man pointed at the tiger bones and told Old Wisdom that he'd like to buy ten grams. Ming weighed out the amount and wrapped it in newspaper. The man lifted the package, bringing it up to his shoulders and then down again. "You sure this is ten grams?" he said. "The scale isn't rigged, is it?"

"No," Old Wisdom said. "Never."

The man smiled. "A joke." He turned to Ming. "If you *are* interested, be sure to come to your high school tomorrow. The assembly is at five."

After the man left, Old Wisdom scolded his son. "How many times do I have to tell you? When we serve someone from the city, we use the real weights."

On his way to his friend's house, Ming was so excited he rode his bike through a rain puddle, mud splashing onto his pants and ankles. Even though the two of them were the same age, Tao was still in high school. He had been held back twice, and unlike Ming, he never had much hope in escaping the village. The two of them were friends because at one point Ming had liked Tao's sister, who now worked as a flight attendant for Air China.

"The man came to my class," Tao said. "He picked three of us to attend the assembly." Tao was half a foot taller than Ming and had the habit of craning his neck when speaking.

"Did he tell you how many people he's taking?"

Tao shook his head. "Interviews will be given tomorrow. He told us that, above all, he was looking for people who were capable of enduring hard labor—healthy people."

Nodding, Ming considered the state of his own health. He had been a long jumper in high school, winning Xinchun's track meet with a record-setting leap of 445 centimeters. Although the condition of his body was far from prime, all the extra fieldwork he had to do because of his absent brothers and old father kept him at least healthy. He flexed his biceps in front of Tao. "You think this body will get me in?" he asked, half jokingly and half self-consciously.

"Maybe," Tao said. "Would've been better if you'd have taken some of your dad's medicine."

Ming folded his arms. "That stuff is worthless."

"That stuff is your livelihood."

The two friends left Tao's yard and rode their bicycles between the apple trees of Tao's family's orchards. They made their way to the bank of the Yellow River, where they'd always gone before important moments to skip rocks and think. Ming had kissed Tao's sister here, underneath a willow, its branches dangling over the churning river. The two of them were barely seventeen. He had known then that she would not be with him for much longer. She was smarter than he was—top 2 percent—and she was the village beauty. For his entire childhood, Ming had thought the two of them would marry. Now he was trying to play catch-up, not even knowing what country she was in.

"If we both made it to the city," Tao said, "and had to pick one thing from the village to take with us, what would you take?" He took off his shoes, socks, and shirt. He stepped into the clay-colored water, cupping a handful and splashing it on his face.

"Nothing," Ming said, picking up a smooth, black stone. "I'd just take myself: my mind and body. I'm done with everything in Xinchun." He arced his hand behind him, pulling the stone back as if his body was a slingshot, and then launched the stone into the river, where, bouncing once, it disappeared into a frothing wave.

Old Wisdom was worried. He was totaling up the day's profits and it occurred to him that he had sold the tiger bones too cheaply. With the cost of shipping and the labor involved in its separation, he should've charged at least five or six *yuan* more per gram. Ming was a smart kid. Why hadn't he caught it? Or, if he had, why hadn't he said anything? *Always thinking about other places, dreaming about a life not meant for him, the boy was careless. And ungrateful*, Old Wisdom thought. If it hadn't been for the store's income, he never would've had enough money to bribe the family-planning commissioner, and Ming would've never been born. Now, like all of his children, the boy planned to abandon him.

Old Wisdom knew the dangers of living outside Xinchun. In crowded cities, life mattered little, especially the life of a young man from the countryside. He had read about factory jobs where bosses worked their staff to the point of exhaustion. The employees lived in the company's houses and ate the company's food, and naturally, the boss controlled when they slept and ate. He might even control the schedule of one's defecation.

Here, in Xinchun, Ming would inherit a store and become a respected member of the community, looked up to by everyone as the village herbalist. The boy didn't understand how good he had it, how hard his father had worked to give him this future.

Old Wisdom took off his glasses and pinched the bridge of his nose. Observing his reflection in his outhouse's mirror, he saw that his beard was growing too long. Strands curled below his neck and touched his collarbone. He would need to trim it soon, else he would look ragged, and nobody would come to his store and trust his prescriptions.

The two men from the city slept in their cars: Zhang Sha, Director of Search, in his Mercedes with the driver seat inclined, and Li Tan, Director of Transportation, in the bed of his truck over a sheepskin blanket. The next day, they waited by the school until classes ended. They bought pickled duck eggs and fried dough from a vendor cart for lunch, and nodded to all the students as they streamed out. Smiling, they stepped on the butts of their cigarettes before going inside.

"Greetings," Zhang Sha said. "You all should be proud for having been selected to attend this assembly."

Li, the larger and darker-colored of the two men, looking like a Mongolian, stood behind him.

The young villagers sat on stools in a semicircle. Ming was glad Tao had also been picked. There were ten of them, and, with the exception of Ming, all were still in high school. The cafeteria was about twice the size of a normal classroom, where grades one through twelve all had lunch. Located in the basement, the room's narrow windows were close to the ceiling. Grease stained the walls.

"We have connections with a variety of companies," Zhang Sha continued. "Some of our people are at hospitals; others have attained jobs in offices, getting paid to sit in a cushiony chair and drink tea all day. It all depends on how smart and dedicated you are, because once you reach the city, we don't want you to have second thoughts. When you don't make money, we don't make money." Zhang paused, taking a sip of hot water from a rusty Thermos. "This is why we offer an extensive training period to assess your potential so that we can fit you with the proper job. Best of all, both you and your family will be paid during this period. We understand that you need money to live in the city, and that your family needs money to hire people to work in your place here in the village."

Ming couldn't believe his good fortune. Now his father couldn't possibly object.

"We only ask one thing," Zhang said, and Ming sank back in his seat, waiting for the catch. "We ask for your dedication. During this training period, which can last for a few months to a year, depending on the person, you will not be allowed to contact your family, your girlfriend, or anyone else who might cause distractions. Simply put, we want you to succeed, and if you back out in the middle of your training, not only will you not succeed, we will have lost money."

After Zhang finished his speech, there was a question-and-answer period. Little Slope, the son of an apricot and pear farmer on

the east side of Xinchun, asked how much money would be given
to his parents when he left. "Five hundred," answered Zhang. "All
up front. That should be more than enough to cover a year's worth
of labor." Parched Well, whose father farmed the lands west of Xinchun's main well, asked how soon they were leaving. "Tomorrow
morning," Zhang said. "We have a strict schedule. Can't waste any
time." Finally, Ming stood up and asked what would happen if, after
the training period, they still couldn't find a job for him. "That has
never happened," Zhang said, picking up his briefcase and taking
out several sheets of paper. "Although if it did, we'd simply drive you
back here. You can think of it as a year-long paid vacation. It's all
explained in the contract."

When there were no more questions, the young villagers lined
up in front of the two men to read and sign the contracts. "Give a
copy to your parents as well," Zhang said. "We can't take you unless
they agree."

Ming and Tao were last in line. The two friends made bets on
who would complete their training first. Then they decided that it'd
be best if they finished at the same time, so that they'd be appointed
to the same company.

"I hope the old man agrees," Ming said. "You're lucky to have a
supportive family."

"Not supportive." Tao shook his head. "They don't care where I
end up. I won't even tell them about the five hundred *yuan*."

"Wish I could do the same. I'm not so sure that money is enough
to convince my old man," Ming said, even though he was fairly certain it would.

His father had married off his sister because the doctor from
Shanghai had come from a wealthy family. In fact, the doctor had
given his father enough money for him to renovate the store, to
install new windows and a new countertop. Ming and his father

barely saw his sister anymore, and his father didn't seem bothered at all. Sometimes Ming wondered if his father loved any of them, if he considered his sons, his daughter, and his wife—when she'd been alive—as anything more than extra hands.

By the time Ming made it back to the store, the line had passed the bicycle racks and reached Lao Mei's DVD and VCD rental shop. Alligator tails were in high demand, known to prevent disease and bring good luck. A few customers, seeing Ming, shouted, "Get me a good deal!" Ming, not bothering to lock his bike, brushed past them and rushed into the store.

"Where were you?" Old Wisdom asked. His hands shook as he scooped the powdered alligator tail onto the scale.

"Let me get that for you." Ming lifted the wooden ledge and went around the counter. With the spoon in hand, he said, "I have something important to talk to you about."

"Later. Not when we're busy."

It was close to ten by the time the last customer was gone. Old Wisdom, exhausted, sat back on his stool and left the door open to let in the summer breeze. He smelled apple blossoms from the orchards, wildflowers along the dirt road, and budding sorghum from the fields. Running an herbal supply store had taught him that this combination of scents was good for his health, that whenever he felt close to nature, nature was rejuvenating him.

Ming took advantage of his father's good mood and set the five hundred *yuan* on the glass tabletop.

"What's this?" Old Wisdom asked.

"This is what I've been trying to tell you. I went to the assembly today. The man from yesterday gave us this money for me to go to the city."

Old Wisdom uncurled the bills, counted them, then laid them back on the tabletop. "Your father may be a cheap man. But five hundred *yuan* isn't enough to buy one of his sons."

"Nobody's buying anyone. I've spoken to Twisted Weasel, the fourteen-year-old son of Mao Bing, and he said he'd gladly help you out in the fields and in the store for only *two* hundred *yuan* a year."

Old Wisdom shook his head. "Those men from the city are crooks. Once they have you, they'll squeeze all the sweat out of you. You don't know how hard city life is."

"They warned us that it's going to be difficult," Ming said. He got on his knees, took his father's hand, and kissed it. "Dad, all my brothers are gone. Tao's sister is gone. And soon, Tao will be gone. What will I have left in Xinchun?"

Making his children happy was never one of Old Wisdom's priorities, but gazing into his son's eyes, which had a film of tears, and feeling how tightly his son held his wrinkled hands, Old Wisdom understood that this was the only thing his son had ever truly wanted, and keeping him in Xinchun was an act too selfish even for an old man like himself.

That night, as Ming was busy packing his bags, Old Wisdom paced in their center yard, outside of his son's room. On occasion, he peeked through the window and saw his son stuffing clothes into two emptied sorghum sacks. They didn't have the time or money to buy proper luggage, and Old Wisdom knew his son would be recognized as a bumpkin as soon as he stepped off the truck. *Well,* he thought, *at least the boy would have a place to eat and sleep.* Who knows? Maybe all the hard work would show him how good he had it in the village. With any luck, he'd be back home in no time.

II.

As the truck ascended the Blood Cloud Mountains, curling along the highway guardrails, a fog settled and Xinchun Village started to disappear. Ming saw fields vanishing under the fog like dreams, like lands winking in and out of reality. That morning, for the first time in years, his father had woken up early. He had cooked for him, prepared him scallion cakes and bean curd in vinegar—dishes his mother used to make—and waited with the other families while the men from the city helped the boys and their luggage up to the truckbed. Only six of the ten boys showed up, and it surprised Ming that the men from the city didn't go to their houses to collect the five hundred *yuan* they had advanced them.

"Can I have a piece of that scallion cake?" Tao asked. "My family didn't prepare anything for me."

They were still twisting up the mountain, the road bumpy underneath, and Ming had trouble tearing off a piece. He handed Tao an unevenly torn wedge, then asked, "When was the last time you went to the city?"

"Last fall," Tao said, "to sell off our extra apple crop. We didn't make a lot of money though; everyone had a good harvest that year. So for an entire month, we ate all our dishes with apples—apple-fried pork, eggs scrambled with apples, dumplings with turnips and apples—and still, we had to throw away half a ton." Biting into the scallion cake, Tao brushed crumbs off his pants, which were still muddy from yesterday's swim. "I'm going to miss Xinchun," he said. "Even if we'll be gone just for a year, I don't know if we're doing the right thing. A lot of people left when we were kids, and watching them get on a bus or tractor with such a huge smile on their faces, I promised myself I'd never be one of them. You think the driver would let me off if I asked him to stop? I can give back the money and walk home."

"Don't be scared. Those people who left were smart. They knew the village had nothing to offer them. Plus, with me gone, what're you going to do in Xinchun? If you stay, at least we'll miss it together."

Tao nodded, but Ming could tell his friend was still unconvinced. "I don't know if I want to work in the city. Like my father used to tell me, it's better to be a big fish in a pond than a big fish in the ocean."

"That would be true," Ming said. "Except we were both little fish, and Xinchun's opportunities, like its wells, have all dried up."

"Would the two of you be quiet?" Little Slope said. He was lying on the truck's wheelbed, his arm over his eyes blocking out the sun, trying to fall asleep.

The mountain path was the only way out of Xinchun Village. It took two hours to travel through it. The poorly paved road merged onto a highway, and when the truck neared the outskirts of Yuncheng City—the roads becoming bogged down—the sky turned gray and polluted. Smoke rose from the local coal refinery and blended with the clouds. Parched Well coughed, his lungs unaccustomed to the polluted air. The truck reached their exit an hour later, where the ramp was completely backed up.

Little Slope awoke and looked around. "What's going on?"

"Traffic," Ming said.

Little Slope tapped on the truck's rear window. "Hey," he shouted, "you in there. How long is this going to take?"

The Mongolian glanced in his rearview mirror, then rolled down his window. "None of your business."

"If it's going to be long, would you mind if we stopped somewhere? I need to pee."

"Sit down," the Mongolian said. "Don't say another word."

Little Slope sat back down on the wheelbed. Ming wondered if this attitude was part of the training or if the Mongolian was just an angry man. Of course, Ming thought, he had been a villager just like them, and the company couldn't find him a job so they had him drive the truck.

"Don't worry about Little Slope," Ming shouted. "He'll understand his place soon enough."

"Who do I look like?" the Mongolian said. "Who do you think I am? Another word from any of you and I'll drive a knife through your face."

Night had fallen hours ago. By the time they reached their destination, Ming could no longer tell what time it was. They were on the other side of Yuncheng, beyond the downtown area with the tall buildings and fancy restaurants, where he had hoped their training facility would be located. Instead, he saw two identical single-floor houses placed side by side, in the back of which there was a warehouse with blackened windows running just below the roof. Beyond the warehouse two rows of tall trees concealed the three structures from the road, and Ming could see faint glimmers of streetlamps and headlights passing through the trees. In front of each building, two or three men stood smoking.

"Leave your things on the truck," Zhang Sha said.

Getting off the truck, the six boys were asked to hold a long, coarse rope. They hesitated, but Zhang assured them that it was a precautionary measure, so they wouldn't get lost when he took them to their rooms. He led at the front, pulling a handle at the end of the rope, while the Mongolian held a similar handle at the rear.

The house they entered was barely furnished. A grocery-store calendar with a girl in a bathing suit hung from a wall, and a single couch—its cushions missing—blocked off the entrance to the kitchen. On it, two men in their undershirts sat eating black-bean noodles and watching a table tennis match on a handheld TV. The only person who stood up when the villagers entered was a middle-aged woman wearing an apron, her belly swollen.

"They're here!" Zhang said. He took out the package of tiger bones from his briefcase and handed it to the woman. "Got this from the village," he whispered. "Should be good for the baby."

The woman gave the villagers a dismissive glance before looking at the package. "You know I don't believe in this stuff. Why do you keep buying it?"

"Take it for me," Zhang said, and then kissed the woman on the forehead.

Together with the two men from the couch, Zhang and the Mongolian led the villagers through the kitchen and then down to the basement, where five pairs of bunk beds filled the space from one wall to the other. Two sleeping men occupied one pair, and a man sat on the bottom bunk of another. A single light bulb illuminated the room. There were two buckets in a corner, and Ming knew immediately, even from the top of the stairs, that they were filled with feces.

"Go down there and join the others," the Mongolian said, taking the rope.

"Please," Zhang added. "Classes will begin tomorrow."

The door slammed before the villagers could move. They made their way down tentatively, lowering their feet one step at a time, the light too dim to make out individual stairs.

Ming had expected the conditions to be bad, but he never dreamed that anyone from the *city* could live like this, worse than even the poorest person in Xinchun Village. He took the bed closest to the three people already in the room, and Tao climbed up to the top bunk.

"This is bad," Tao said.

Ming nodded. He stared at the man in front of him, an old villager, forty or fifty, bare-chested, wearing only a pair of tattered trousers, and the man stared back with a grin on his face. "How are the classes?" Ming asked.

"Classes?" The man laughed. "You still believe there are going to be classes?" The bed partially blocked the light, and only half of his face was illuminated. "This is a place to die." He paused. "That's right. You are all going to die."

The other villagers gathered around Ming and Tao's bunk. "What do you mean?" Parched Well asked.

"He's crazy," Little Slope said.

"Your friends seem peaceful enough." Ming pointed to the occupied bunk beds behind the man.

"Hey," Little Slope shouted, "you there sleeping. Wake up. Is your friend crazy?"

The man stopped grinning. He seemed to have regretted opening his mouth. "Leave them be. They're here by choice. Like me, they sold their organs."

Ming saw a cut on the right side of the man's body. As if sheared by scissors, it stretched from his ribcage to the bottom of his belly.

"That's right," the man said, following Ming's gaze. "They're taking out my other kidney in a week. The big man, the one who drives the truck, he tells me they're going to gouge out my eyes, too."

"This can't be true," Tao said.

"We're here to find jobs," said Ming. "This is a training facility."

The old man shook his head. "I'm sorry. I don't know what came over me. I shouldn't have laughed at your misfortune. I've been here too long."

"I have to get out of here," Little Slope said.

The others, stricken, backed away from the man. Parched Well tripped over a bucket of feces. Little Slope ran up the stairs, and the rest of the villagers followed. They crowded around the door. Ming and Tao moved up to the front. "Open up!" Tao shouted, pounding on the door. "We want out!" Ming felt his legs growing weak as he tried turning the knob. Then there was a shove from behind, and his cheek was pressed against the cold steel of the door.

They heard footsteps. "Stop it," someone on the other side said. But this only urged them on. They were making progress. The door began to bulge. Just when they felt they needed one more push, it opened. Ming saw three men standing in front of him—the Mongolian and the two men from the couch. They pushed the villagers back, attempting to re-close the door. Ming felt a kick to his stomach. Undaunted, he pushed past them and ran through the kitchen. He leapt over the couch, glancing back to see a man pursuing him. He opened the front door. Another man was there waiting, and before Ming could run out, the butt of a rifle came crashing into his face.

He heard it distinctly: music. Violins, French horns, and timpani, building and cascading like clouds during a storm, the raindrops in the air refracting light into rainbows. He thought he was dreaming. The last time Ming heard this rendition of *The Butterfly Lovers*, he had been visiting his sister in Shanghai. He had hoped her husband, the doctor, would give him a job in his hospital. "Do you have any experience?" the doctor asked, and Ming told him about helping his father at the store, weighing and mixing herbal medicine, memorizing his father's prescriptions. The doctor shook his head. "No, that won't do. I'm afraid you'll need some real medical training." And his sister smiled at him, and then hummed along with the melody. She wore nice clothes—a sunflower dress, jet-colored hair clips, and sequined shoes—and Ming thought she looked just as pretty as Tao's sister the day she had left Xinchun. No one would've guessed that his sister was from the countryside, that the two of them were related.

When Ming woke up, he was no longer in the basement. It took him a few seconds to realize that he was inside a cage. The cage, designed for some kind of dangerous animal, was inside a warehouse, and it extended halfway up to the ceiling, where round halogen lamps made everything in the room glow a sterile white. The music was coming from a stereo ten or fifteen meters away. Next to it, several doctors circled an operation table. They wore square hats and green scrubs. Their gloves were a splattered pink, almost floral. Their white masks moved when they talked.

"This one is going to America," one of them said. "We expect extra compensation."

Another doctor lifted a brown organ in the shape of a bean seemingly out of the table, held it up to the light, and then placed it into a white Styrofoam box. "Refrigerator," he told the man next to him.

Sitting on a chair a few meters away from the table was the Mongolian, and when Ming noticed him, the big man smiled and walked over. "See anything you like?" he asked. "Only costs you a million or so *yuan* to buy a kidney, more for a liver or a pair of lungs. Soon you will need them all."

Suddenly, a loud noise drew Ming's attention to the other side of the warehouse. Next to the driveway, where a truck was docked, a stone furnace churned. There was a belt feeding a body into the furnace. Ming couldn't be sure, but he thought the body's long neck belonged to Tao.

"Just like you," the Mongolian said. "Liked to make trouble, so we picked him to process first."

Behind the furnace, hiding in half-darkness, a body hung from a hook. Its eyes were gouged out and there was a hole under the ribcage where the stomach and intestines were supposed to be. The boy had long legs. His head rested on his collarbone, and his big toe, almost touching the floor, was blistered from walking in fields. Maybe it was what the Mongolian had just said, but as Ming cried, the only thought that came to his mind was how much potential the boy had had. The boy had the ideal body for a long jumper. With training and luck, he was sure the boy could've beaten his own record of 445 centimeters.

Since Ming's absence, Old Wisdom's days had become long and difficult. Twisted Weasel was the laziest boy he'd ever seen, equally bad at tilling the fields as he was at weighing and mixing medicine. Old Wisdom missed his son, who he hoped missed him too. Harvest time was coming up, and without Ming's help, he was unsure if he'd get through the season. The profits from the store weren't enough. Soon he might have to sell it. What then could he pass down when his son returned? Ming would be penniless, one of those landless peasants in the village who begged for food.

No, it wasn't too late. He'd collect all the sorghum himself if he had to, sacrificing his body, if it meant that his son would retain his position in Xinchun. What did his tired, shriveled body matter anyway when it came to his son's future?

With renewed vigor, he returned to the task at hand: filling out new orders of tiger bones. The task, like most tasks, had been Ming's responsibility, and Old Wisdom remembered his son's complaint the last time he had to do it. Ming had told him that they should stop supplying tiger bones, because tigers were becoming extinct. "Nonsense," Old Wisdom had explained. "Most of these tigers were bred in captivity, with the sole purpose of providing the world with their bones."

In any case, now wasn't the time to think about tigers. He had his own problems. On the paper, in the blank indicating weight, he wrote down twenty kilograms, which was double the amount of the last shipment. He put the order in the mailbox. He hoped that it would arrive soon and without delay.

THE WHOLE STORY OF A TUGBOAT DRIVER ON SUZHOU RIVER

—Why was he a hero?

After fishing a woman's hand out of Suzhou River, he helped to solve a murder case.

—Wait. How did he find the hand?

He was driving his tugboat upriver, pulling a barge full of garbage. It was raining that day and he was playing with his Captain America, Wolverine, and Spiderman toys. He didn't know who or what they were, but he liked them; he imagined that anything American boys had must be of the highest quality. He tied them to a ball of Styrofoam and pretended that they were his crew and that his tugboat was sinking. "Abandon ship!" he called out, but his crew didn't listen. So he tossed them overboard. Then he took out his long fisherman's net and fished them out of the oily water.

Fishing out Wolverine, he saw the woman's hand. It was bobbing

THE WHOLE STORY OF A TUGBOAT DRIVER ON SUZHOU RIVER

on the surface, like the top of an iceberg, as if the rest of the body was hiding below. He fished it out and placed it beside the steering wheel. For the next week, he examined it thoroughly. From the smooth nails and skinny fingers, he could tell it once belonged to a girl. One day, as he was looking at Wolverine and Captain America, he wondered if Old Man in the Sky, sending him the hand, was giving him a sign. Like his shipwrecked crew, anyone missing a hand was also in need of saving. And so he couldn't stop dreaming about the girl. He drew pictures of her face and body to match the hand. She was a small girl, he was sure, with a skinny waist and a long neck. At the end of the week, he wrapped the hand in newspaper and turned it over to the police. The following month, they found the body.

The other tugboat drivers had made fun of him—playing with toys. Now, he was a hero.

—Why did he like toys so much?

When he was a boy in the countryside, he couldn't get enough of toys, but his family farmed and didn't have much money. His father had served under the Communist Liberation Army and was a veteran of Korea and Vietnam. He wanted his son to join the army, too, and make a name for the Yang family. As soon as Yang turned seventeen, his father put him on a bus heading for a military barrack. But Yang was too much of a prankster. He didn't take anything seriously. When the bus stopped at Shanghai, he got off, and since then, never spoke to his parents again.

Thinking back to those times, he was reminded of how lucky he was now. Every day, he drove with Captain America, Wolverine, and Spiderman taped to his deck. The kids around Shanghai all knew and liked him because he gave them toys. He saved the best toys for the holidays, and during the Spring Festival, he'd carry a sack over his shoulders, dump the toys on the deck of his boat, and give the kids anything they wanted.

It made him happy, seeing the children so excited. And the toys didn't cost him a *fen*.

—*What else did he see, driving his tugboat?*

He saw everything along the river. Every evening, he returned to port and passed under some twenty or thirty bridges. Their shadows fell on his tugboat and slowly crawled up his deck and everything became dark for a few seconds, then it was light again. And then he passed under another bridge, and then another, the sun going down, the sky turning from blue to orange to red, until there was no longer any difference between bridge and sky.

—*Let's go back to the free toys. Where did he get them?*

On Wednesdays, he stopped by a toy factory on the far west side of Shanghai and there he found large quantities of discarded action figures and toy guns and dolls. He couldn't understand why the factory had thrown them out. They all seemed fine to him. Why couldn't they have saved the toys and given them to the children in the city? There were many orphanages in Shanghai, and a lot of children had nothing—no relatives, no possessions, no future.

On Wednesdays, he lugged the toys all the way back to the other side of Shanghai. At night, he spent his time separating the ones he liked from the ones he'd throw away. The other tugboat drivers saw him on his boat digging through blacks bags and laughed at him. They told him that he was a child. He didn't pay them any attention. The look on the children's faces during the holidays made up for their ridicule.

Eventually, the parents heard about what he was doing. He had not yet become a hero, so the more well-to-do parents thought he was dangerous and forbade their children from going to a garbage boat and accepting gifts from a strange man. The poorer parents sometimes came along with their children, and out of gratitude gave Yang dumplings and noodles and moon cakes. In return, he gave them toys as well.

—So he collected garbage?
Every day, he picked up garbage from the ceramics factory, the fish shops, the pharmaceuticals, and the wealthy residential apartments. He put the garbage on his barge and pulled it from one side of Shanghai to the other. At the end of each day, he smelled like some combination of rotten eggs, feces, soda pop, and fresh plastic. It wasn't a glorious job, and he had difficulty finding a girl.

But that wasn't even the whole story. Sometimes his barge would become too full and he was forced to dump garbage on the deck of his tugboat. When he first became a tugboat driver, he didn't know how to pack the garbage on his deck and sometimes it would seep through the bridge and into his living quarters. In the morning, he occasionally found himself drenched in watermelon juices, pork blood, and urine.

There was a lot more to running a tugboat, he found out, than just picking up and hauling trash. The subtleties took him years to learn.

—Where did he get the tugboat in the first place?
When he first arrived in Shanghai, Yang sold imported Russian vodka on the streets. He rode a motorcycle and carried a gun. He was young.

One day, a business partner sold him out to the cops. He got two years for possessing and soliciting illegal imported items. When he got out, he became a beggar and slept on the streets. He was nothing more than garbage. One winter day, hungry and frostbitten, Yang found himself sleeping in a trashcan. The next morning, he awoke on a tugboat with an old man by his side feeding him medicine. He and the old man became friends, and then he became the old man's apprentice. When the old man died two years later, he bequeathed to Yang his boat and his livelihood. From then on, Yang lived the life the old man had lived.

One of his former business partners, seeing that Yang now had a boat, offered to join forces again. When Yang refused, the man sent his gang at night to teach him a lesson. The man beat Yang and set his boat on fire. In the morning, the other tugboat drivers helped him to extinguish the fire. After the incident, the tugboat drivers made a vow to help each other.

He was not a hero yet, so the tugboat drivers gave him the least desirable territory on the river, from Xuhui District where the river was shallow, to Songjiang District where the river ended. Yang didn't mind. He was grateful that they had saved his life and accepted him into their community. He hadn't felt so lucky since he had left the countryside. Now, he had a legal occupation in the city.

—*So what was driving a tugboat like?*

At first, he found the tugboat noisy. The engine's churning never ceased and he felt his eardrums growing numb. But as he got used to the noise, he started finding the daily journey back and forth across the river solemn. You had to know where to pay attention. You had to stop listening to the engine and look at the scenery. The bridges, for example.

The bridges hung low towards the river, and at first, Yang was afraid they'd hit the top of his boat. They were the spots during the day where vendors sold vases and T-shirts and lighters on top of picnic mats, and also the spots during the night where beggars slept. It was where the old tugboat driver had found him, frostbitten inside a garbage can.

Now every time he passed under a bridge he would look up and see what the old man once saw: people buying gifts from the picnic merchants during the day, their bags swaying between the iron girdles; or beggars sleeping on the same mats during the night, their slippers protruding between the stone handlebars.

He saw the beggars on the bridges, especially during winter, and often wondered why the old tugboat driver had chosen him. There were so many people he could have saved—so many in need of saving—that he sometimes felt at once lucky and undeserving that so generous a man had chosen him instead of the other, and probably more worthy, beggars. Most of them were natives of the city—had birth certificates to prove it—and it didn't feel right to Yang that he, someone from the countryside, took away one of their rightful jobs.

—Did he always drive his tugboat alone? Did he ever marry?

Before putting him on the bus to the barrack, his parents had engaged him to a girl. They were to get married after he had seen the world. She was the butcher's daughter, light with an airy kind of beauty. When he grew older and had long given up on finding a wife, he could still remember tugging on her two black braids and the way she had giggled afterwards. He remembered stealing slabs of pork and beef from her father's butcher shop and letting her father catch him because she was one of the prettiest girls in the village. The old butcher punished anybody who stole from him by making the youngster work in his butcher shop chopping meat for the entire weekend. He thought his punishment was harsh enough, but he kept wondering why so many boys still kept stealing. His daughter was picky and only brought water and food for a few of the boys that were caught. Yang thought he was one of the few, if not the only boy, who the old butcher's daughter liked. Other kids bragged that they had their way with her too, but he knew they were lying.

After coming to the city and becoming a tugboat driver, he found out that no woman in Shanghai would talk to him. They told him he looked and smelled like a cow carcass. He wondered how the other tugboat drivers found wives. So he asked them if they could introduce him to some women. The other tugboat drivers' wives introduced him to their sisters and cousins and he went out with them a couple of times, but they were ugly, and he considered himself above them.

Then one day, he had to pick up one of the tugboat driver's daughters from school. Her name was Dai Dai. She walked around the dock like she owned the place. She was a young girl but had already developed into a woman, and she didn't mind the stench of his tugboat since she was used to her father's. She thought he was handsome. When he picked her up from school that day, the other kids were making fun of her because she was the daughter of a tugboat driver. He comforted her, held her in his arms, and told her not to listen to her friends, that she was actually very lucky. They kissed, and then made love. This went on for a few weeks. Then Dai Dai started wearing perfume and short skirts, and soon after decided to leave him. He was heartbroken and couldn't sleep and thought about her every day. He drove as close to land as possible so that he could wave to her when she walked to school. She ignored him, but he caught the attention of some of her friends.

He didn't force the girls to do anything, and they sometimes brought their friends. Some of the boys even came on his boat to smoke cigarettes and drink beer. They had parties after school.

At these parties, Yang felt like a kid again, like he was back in the countryside. Later on, the older kids brought along their younger brothers and sisters, and Yang stockpiled water pistols and dolls and other expensive American toys.

—If he couldn't find love in the city, why didn't he go back to the countryside?

More than once, he thought about going back, but his parents would have passed away long ago. And although curious, he also wanted to keep that same image of the girl from his village in his head. He knew he'd be disappointed if he ever went back. Anyway, he was well-liked on Suzhou River. After he had helped to solve the murder case, he was a hero.

—Was he happy?

He spent most of his nights alone on his tugboat, fishing the Suzhou River. He never caught anything, though. The river was man-made, dank, and greasy, and had long ago lost its ability to support life. Sometimes Yang thought about committing suicide. He didn't want to drown himself, though, because he remembered how terrible it had all been: the police dragging the body out of the river with the tall forklift stationed on the nearby bridge, the beggars watching, the pedestrians, occasionally glancing over, continuing to buy their T-shirts and lighters as if nothing had happened.

—Why did he feel so bad?

After Yang had fished the severed hand out of the water and the police had found the rest of the body, he asked if he could see it. He went to the morgue and saw the rest of the girl. It was a young woman, small and lithe. But the face resembled something he had almost forgotten: Dai Dai. The severed hand, lying next to the arm, didn't quite match. It was white, whereas the body was more green and black because of the river's toxins seeping deep into the skin. Yang slid the hand next to the arm, checking to make sure they matched. He saw that the width of the wrist was identical to that of the forearm. Still, the hand looked too fresh for the rest of the body. He wondered how long the hand and the body had been apart, and why the killer thought it necessary to remove it, since he left the other arms and legs attached. And why did the hand retain its whiteness when the rest of the body turned green? They had both been soaking in the polluted waters of the Suzhou River. Why did the color of the hand differ from the color of the body?

The authorities had assured him the girl was not from Shanghai, that she was a party leader's daughter from Beijing who had run away from home and ended up with a gang on Suzhou River, but he felt responsible for her death. He thought it was Old Man in the Sky's justice. The tugboat drivers looked up to him, but he was overcome with guilt. Besides making him a hero, the hand, he believed, was returning for revenge, wanting to make him suffer.

—*Did he tell anybody about what the hand meant to him?*

Nobody knew. At his funeral, the children all remembered him as Mr. Yang, the lonely tugboat man who gave them toys. The other tugboat drivers had no idea either. They pitched in and gave him a large funeral in the traditional manner. They invited the grade school children to come and the children each placed a toy he had given them around his body. Circled by superheroes and dolls, he traveled the length of the river one last time, his body in shadow each time it passed under a bridge.

—*If the kids called him Mr. Yang, then Yang was his last name. What was his first name?*

He was from the countryside, where everybody believed if Old Man in the Sky found out your newborn's full name within the first few years of its life, he could claim their soul. The deaths of babies were common in the countryside, and parents gave them ugly nicknames like Pig Feces and Foot Fungus and Rotten Rice. Old Man in the Sky, unwilling to admit into heaven such horrid names, would leave their children alone.

When Yang turned six, his parents brought in the village sage to help them pick out a real name for Yang. Until that point, they had called him "Dirty Bowl." They must choose Yang's real name carefully. If your name doesn't suit your own destiny, Old Man in the Sky would become confused and set you on a crooked path.

It was the sage's job to predict the boy's future. The sage studied Yang's teeth and feet and the swirls in his hair and told his parents. He did not predict that Yang was going to become a hero. He said, "Your son is going to live a plain life. He will be a traditional man, simple and kind." He predicted good harvests but heavy rains. "Very heavy rains," he repeated. "Perhaps even floods."

"What should his name be?"

The sage stroked his beard and looked away. Then he shook his head.

"What?" his parents asked. "What do you see? Is he going to be fortunate, sorrowful, gentle, mean, hardworking, or lazy? Please, give us a word."

The sage turned around.

"Yes," he said, which told them everything.

A FAMILY ACCIDENT

I was thirteen when Bao Meng'er kidnapped me. This was almost forty years ago. Back then, he had a habit of snatching up boys from neighboring fields and forcing them to work in his place in his family's squash racks, while he slept on a tractor drinking sweet potato wine and eating hare jerky. He was tall, scar-faced, and bare-chested. He wore camouflaged pants and a fur-lined hunting cap, his muscles as tight and coarse as mule-hair rope. He called me Little Peanut and punched me in the gut before letting me go home. A year later, his aunt had the nerve to knock on our door and ask my mother for a marriage prospect with my older sister. I was furious. I yelled, "Just because Mishu isn't as smart as everyone else doesn't mean she should marry someone like Bao Meng'er!" My mother silenced me. In truth, she'd been worried about my sister's future for quite a while. Mishu, twenty-five at the time, was four years older than Bao Meng'er. No one had come to our door asking for her hand. Our family was poor and Mishu was stupid.

The Meng'er family was famous in Xinchun Village for their swindling past. During the late 1800s, right after the Qing Dynasty collapsed, Great-Grandpa Meng'er opened an antique store in which he and his sons sold counterfeit *Qing* coins, their motto: *Buy so that your children will be rich!* During the Cultural Revolution, Grandpa Meng'er led a cadre of Red Guards through Xinchun's streets, plucking villagers from their yards for ten *yuan* a head, denouncing them for indecent behavior. It didn't surprise anyone that Bao, the oldest Meng'er boy, found himself without a marriage prospect. He carried a carving knife tucked in his belt wherever he went. He and his brothers stole from Old Wisdom's medicine shop and spat on the doorstep of the village chief.

My sister ended up agreeing to the marriage. The entire village came to the wedding. It was a spectacle: the least eligible maiden marrying the least eligible bachelor. We lit firecrackers, chewed on dried octopus, and did cartwheels along the street. As Bao Meng'er and his gang of brothers—my future cousins—paraded through the neighborhood banging gongs and throwing confetti, they gave each boy under twelve a wooden gun that fired rubber bands. I felt sorry for my sister, who must've been confused and frightened, her face under a red veil, a gigantic paper rose covering her stomach, her hand clinging to a long golden rod connecting her to her future husband, without whom she wouldn't know which way to walk.

A year later, my father pushed me to marry the daughter of one of his World War II buddies. I didn't want to protest, both because Confucius told us to always listen to our parents and because there wasn't anyone I was interested in. My wife and I had a boy and a girl, and after our daughter married a man from a neighboring village, we moved in with our son and daughter-in-law. My wife got along with them fine, but it seemed like a lot of the time the three of them didn't remember that I was around. Sometimes I would take an afternoon nap and nobody would call me for dinner. I would wake up to find the three of them munching on fish cakes and rice or slurping black bean noodles. There'd only be three chairs circling the square wooden table in our center yard.

"Forget me again?" I would say, pulling up a stool.

"Don't be silly," my wife would say. "How can anyone forget an old man who likes to sleep all day?"

"Who can forget the cost of such an old man's arthritis medicine?" my son would add.

They'd laugh, and I'd laugh, too. Then I'd try to put it all in the back of my mind. I was just being sensitive. After all, I was family, and nobody could ever forget family.

Bao and Mishu had five boys. The boys became five strong, smart, and capable young men, shattering the long tradition of Meng'er crooks. Two left and found fortune in Yuncheng City, and the three who remained got married and started families of their own here in Xinchun. Most families partitioned their land when their sons married, but even at the time of his youngest son's wedding, Bao Meng'er kept all his land for himself. The three remaining Meng'er boys pleaded with the village chief to persuade their father to give them their share, and it was only after the district police threatened Bao Meng'er with an expensive fine that the old man surrendered. He was forced to pass down his land and house to his children, and he and my sister lived with one son one month and another son another month. This lasted for almost a decade, until all three of their sons started losing patience. Who wanted to live with a rude father and a mother as smart as a child?

On Bao Meng'er sixty-seventh birthday, he and Mishu found themselves with nowhere else to go, thrown out of their youngest son's yard because Bao had slaughtered a lamb without his daughter-in-law's permission. Drunk, he pounded on my door. Mishu carried their belongings in a knapsack over her shoulder.

"Open up, Little Peanut! I see your light on. It's cold out here!"

It was one in the morning. My wife and I had been asleep for hours. The glow he was seeing probably came from our furnace. I put on my slippers and reached for our flashlight. Outside, the air smelled like skunks. Wading through our center yard—my knees hurt from arthritis—I covered my hands with my sleeves to protect them from the shrill winter wind. I opened the window on our front door and shined our flashlight through. Bao Meng'er, his hands still as quick as a tiger's, reached in and took it.

"Shining a light into someone's face," he said. He aimed the flashlight back at me. "How do you like it, Little Peanut?"

"What do you want?"

"My bastard sons have all betrayed me. It'd be your honor to have Mishu and I stay with you."

Sleet covered the dirt road outside. My ankles, exposed, felt like they were submerged in frigid water. Icicles hung from the tops of the limestone wall enclosing our yard.

I yawned. "Just apologize for whatever you did. I'm sure they'll let you back in."

"Kings don't apologize to servants. Fathers don't apologize to sons," he said. "The words of Confucius."

"You've read Confucius."

"Such axioms are understood by all." He shattered his beer bottle on the ground, then gave the door another shove. "Stop stalling, Little Peanut. Let us in. Can't you see your sister's fingers are frost-bitten?"

Mishu waved, her nose dripping snot, and the knapsack fell to the ground. "Hello, little brother."

"Sloppy as a wingless bat." Bao Meng'er picked up the knapsack. "I'm drunk and I still have more sense."

"All right," I said. "My daughter-in-law wouldn't mind Mishu coming in. But we don't have enough room for you. This isn't my yard anymore, either."

"Won't let me in?" Bao said. "Your ancestors can fuck a turtle."

Mishu spat on her hands, then rubbed the warm liquid onto her face. Such actions were cute when we were kids, but now frozen saliva hung from her wrinkled forehead, and she looked like a corpse.

"Well?" Bao Meng'er said to her. "What are you waiting for? Go inside."

Mishu shook her head. "Both of us," she said.

"Don't worry, Cattle Brain. I'll be fine out here. You'll see me in the morning." He unwrapped the knapsack, revealed a stained bed sheet, and began pitching a tent.

I unlocked the door and opened it to a slit. Mishu squeezed in. When we reached the house, she took out an extra blanket from underneath the stone bed. She walked back to the front door and slid it through the window. Then she came inside, undressed, lay at the end of the bed, and fell asleep with the blanket over her face, her gray hair jutting out like stalks of sun-hardened sorghum.

That night, I couldn't tell how well the rest of my family slept, but I barely got a snooze in. Bao Meng'er didn't make it easy on us. He howled an old country song, distorting a lot of the lines:

> Ah, spring roses. Ah, autumn cherry blossoms.
> Ah, the night sky. Ah, the round moon.
> You will be here, you will be here, and you will be here.
> Where will I be when winter is near?

Except for the hourly buses to and from Yuncheng City, cars drove on Xinchun's streets mostly during the morning. Since it was winter, delivery trucks, tractors, and the pastel-colored motorcycles of village boys were parked in ditches, meters away from fallowing fields. The drivers left for work all at once, and from seven to ten, Xinchun's dusty cobbled main street became as packed as a city avenue. When I was little, the morning rooster had woken me up. These days, I got out of bed to honking horns.

Like my son and his wife, Mishu slept late. I had liked to sleep late as well when I was young, but now the only time I had any energy was in the morning.

Bao Meng'er was still behind our front door when I went out to sprinkle salt on our center yard and shovel away the sleet.

"I'm hungry!" he shouted. "Tell Mishu to wake up and bring me something to eat!"

I uncovered our wok and scooped the leftover squid stir-fry into a chipped ceramic bowl. Then I passed it through the front door window.

"Thanks," he said. "Here's your flashlight back." He wolfed down the stir-fry, shoveling the rice into his mouth with his hands, licking strands of carrot and celery off his beard. "Fuck my sons. Fuck their wives. Fuck this village. Little Peanut, you're the only good person left in the world."

"All right," I said.

"I'm serious. I haven't been very kind to you in this lifetime. But, by Buddha, I swear I'll repay all my debts in the next one. If I'm born an ox, I'll clear your fields. If I'm a dog, I'll watch your house. If I'm a sparrow, I'll make my nest above your door and sing your children songs."

"Revolutionary tunes only."

"It's a promise." He wiped his mouth with his sleeve, then

cleaned his beard with a comb. Glancing around like a fox, he gave off the impression that he was about to do something important. "Say goodbye to Mishu for me."

"Where're you going?"

Across the street, our neighbor flung a bag of garbage over his wall. In the distance, smoke rose from the coal refinery and billowed up to the see-through moon.

Bao Meng'er stepped out into the street, turned to me, and waved. "Goodbye, Little Peanut, my only friend!"

"What're you doing?" I tried to unlock the door but my hand jittered. I dropped the key. When I reached down to grab it, my knuckles scraped against a loose wooden panel and my index finger started to bleed.

By the time I made it to the road, Bao Meng'er was lying unconscious on the ground, his cheek against the icy cobblestone. A thin stream of red colored the hair on his upper lip. I had my finger in my mouth, sucking the blood in, and it almost seemed like I was tasting his blood and not my own, that I was the one lying there in front of a rusty green minivan with a crowd of people gathered around.

The ancestors used to say that dragons gave birth to dragons and phoenixes to phoenixes, but a rat could only teach her offspring how to dig holes. Almost an ancestor myself, I lacked such clever sayings. I could only describe how things happened.

My wife, my son, and Mishu were already up when the minivan hit Bao Meng'er. Mishu rushed out with a toothbrush hanging from her mouth. She got down on her knees and shook her husband, whose head bent back like a hose. The driver of the minivan, a tourist guide from the city, introduced himself to me as Mr. Jiang, and phoned the nearest hospital in Yuncheng.

"Is he dead?" my son asked me.

"What happened?" my wife said.

"I don't know. One minute he was talking about dogs and sparrows and the next he was lying on the ground."

"What happened to your hand?" my wife asked.

I nodded to the door. "Need to get that thing replaced."

Mishu kept on shaking her husband. My son tried to pull her aside but she was as sturdy as a brick on the Great Wall. Weeping, she babbled in a language no one understood: long mournful howls followed by teethy bursts of pitter-patter.

Then, miraculously, Bao Meng'er woke up.

"Ouch," he said, rubbing the back of his head.

"Bao Meng'er, you're an elephant." My son laughed. He pulled me aside and whispered, "It's a good thing he didn't die in front of our house."

I wondered if my son would've said the same if it had been my body lying there.

Mr. Jiang squatted next to Bao and patted him on the shoulder. He took off his blue cap with the word DRIVER written on it in English and revealed a round face drenched in sweat. "How about a trip to the hospital?" he asked Bao.

Bao Meng'er spat on the ground. "It's the least you can do, isn't it, you fart-brained lunatic. My leg feels like it's been snapped in two."

"Now wait a minute. You stepped out into the street. You didn't move."

"Tell that to the cops. Come on, Little Peanut, help me up to the van." He motioned me over. "You're coming as a witness. We'll make sure this blind cheetah never drives again."

"I'll do whatever you want," Mr. Jiang said, raisings his arms. "I don't want any trouble."

Mishu and I shared a seat in the back while Jiang drove the van

out of Xinchun Village, up through the Blood Cloud Mountains—
the road so slippery we hit the railing twice—and then onto the
paved highway that led to Yuncheng City. I wasn't comfortable in
such a cushiony seat, and sat using a Tai Chi technique I had learned
from Floating Paper, Xinchun's martial arts master, that put most of
the weight on my legs. Bao Meng'er fell asleep immediately, snoring
along the way. Mishu stroked his hair and pinched his cheeks as if
he was a fat, wrinkled, salivating doll.

"How could you live with him for so long?" I asked.

Mishu stuck out her tongue and slapped the top of her head. She
always did this when she was happy.

"Why are you so happy?" I asked.

"I like the city. Tall buildings. Sweet smell on the street. Meat
vendors. I like to be there because I like to eat."

As soon as we reached the hospital, Mr. Jiang wanted to leave.
Bao Meng'er yelled, "Murderer!" and Jiang let him keep the keys
to the van until the police arrived. The nurses dropped Bao into
a wheelchair and pushed him to a ward painted half-orange. On a
three-legged nightstand, fake dandelions rested in a plastic vase.
The hospital had a sweet smell to it, like that of rice liquor.

I watched them from a bench outside their room and listened to
the doctors as they examined Bao's body. They determined that he
had a concussion and that his right leg was shattered in three places.
Mr. Jiang paced up and down the hallway, occasionally peering out
a window to see if the police had arrived. There were two beds in
the room, and Mishu lay on the other one, pushing the button that
made the mattress bend.

When the doctors left, Bao Meng'er yelled, "Come inside, Little
Peanut. I want to talk to you."

I walked into the room.

"Close the door."

I closed it and sat on the stool in between Bao Meng'er and my sister's beds. "I know what you want from me," I said. "But I'm not going to lie for you."

"Listen to me, Little Peanut. We're family. We've been family for almost forty years. Anyway, I didn't ask you in to talk about that. I want to tell you what I saw back there right before that van hit me." He closed his eyes, breathed in, breathed out, then opened his eyes. "I saw the meaning of life."

There was a sudden chill in the room, like the moment right before I went to bed each night, when the last light was turned off and my eyes hadn't adjusted to the darkness.

"You saw the meaning of life," I repeated.

"Yes. For years I've lived with your sister and I've wondered. I would look at her and I would wonder why she liked living so much. She's sixty-six, four years older than me, but she has as much enthusiasm for life as a ten-year-old."

I turned around and glanced at Mishu. She was on her stomach, her arms and legs spread to the corners of the bed.

"It's not so hard to understand," I said. "My sister likes her life because she has a husband and five sons. What more could she ask for?"

"Let me finish." Bao Meng'er took a sip from the tea that the nurse had poured for him. "Your sister—my wife—she likes to live because she has no concept of death. She has heard of it, of course, but unlike the two of us, she doesn't know that death will come to her as well. When a lion kills a deer, does it think about its own demise years later? Death by old age is an experience almost exclusively reserved for man. Old Man in the Sky made sure of that. But we have to think like the animals—without care—especially given our age, or we'd be so depressed we all might try what I pulled this morning."

Tilting my head, I considered his words. Finally, I managed to say, "I don't think what you just said is the meaning of life."

He picked his nose with his pinky. "It's close."

After going into the hospital and getting Bao Meng'er's testimony, the police pulled Mr. Jiang into their cruiser and questioned him. The poor man came out looking as if he'd just exited a sauna, using a hanky to wipe his forehead before replacing it in his breast pocket. I noticed for the first time that his western-style jacket had patches on the elbow—hand-sewn ones made with festive red tablecloth. He walked over to the grass beside the glossy jade sign that had "Yuncheng City Hospital" written in careful golden calligraphy. Then he squatted down next to me.

"What bad luck," he said. "I had to cancel on three customers today, three rich students from America who wanted to see your village. And now the police won't believe a word I say because my license expired. You know how expensive it is to renew a license these days."

He might've been trying to flatter me. Few villagers had cars, and by my Chairman-Mao cap and cotton-stuffed dungarees, I didn't look like the type to own one.

I said, "I've never driven a car in my life."

"Take pity on me, Old Timer. Just like you, I was born into a poor family. I never knew who my father was. I have a wife and daughter, and my mother is sick with cancer. Every month, her medical bills alone cost me a week's wage. You saw what happened back there. The police will believe you if you just tell them the truth."

As he spoke, a dozen bumpkins pulled up in front of the hospital on a tractor dragging a two-wheeled wagon. Diesel filled our noses.

The bumpkins unlatched the wagon, and two young men carried an unconscious elderly woman into the hospital on a straw-and-bamboo stretcher.

"How old are you?" I asked Jiang.

"I'll be thirty-five this May."

"When I was your age, I never got sick. I could drink all night and still be fresh enough in the morning to plow the sorghum field. My mother, in all her forty-five years, never tasted honey. My first child, a girl, died when she was seven because of diabetes. Even if I believed what you said, me pitying you is like a cricket pitying a panda."

He stretched out his legs, kneaded his calves, and stood up. "You country folks are all the same," he said. "All a bunch of hooligans." He walked through the revolving door and into the hospital.

The police waved me over. There were two of them. They wore brown gloves, they had their pants tucked in their boots, and their leather jackets squeaked whenever they raised their arms. The fat one opened the door to their cruiser, and the skinny one got in next to me. The fat one sat up front, turning around so that his elbows hugged the headrest.

"How long have you known the victim?" he asked.

"All my life. I even know about his family's history. They've lived in Xinchun Village for centuries."

The skinny one wrote down my words on a notepad. When he finished, the fat one asked, "How would you describe your relationship with Bao Meng'er?"

I tucked my hands underneath my thighs and leaned back. "He's my brother-in-law. He treats my sister poorly. Once, when I was a boy, he threw me into the Yellow River. That day, I learned how to swim."

"So you wouldn't call your relations with Bao Meng'er a friend-ship?"

"He's my brother-in-law," I repeated.

The fat one nodded, reached into his pocket, and offered me a cigarette. I took it, and he cupped his palms to light it. For the second time, the skinny one finished scribbling down "brother-in-law."

"Mr. Jiang told us he saw a tent next to your front door," the fat one said. "Why was Bao Meng'er outside your yard this morning?"

"His son had kicked him out. He and my sister came to our door in the middle of the night but we only had enough room on our bed for one more person."

"So you would describe Bao Meng'er's mood this morning as one of agitation."

"He was hungry, so I gave him some rice." I paused, extending my hand to take a better look at the cigarette I was smoking. Its quality surprised me. My lungs felt warm and full, as if they belonged to a much younger man. My mind swam with memories both good and bad. It was true that, until today, Bao Meng'er had not been very kind to me. But he was still my brother-in-law, and I couldn't deny that he played a large part in my life, just as I couldn't deny that Mishu and I came from the same womb, however much I had wanted to when I'd been young. Plus, the old people used to say: when in a complicated situation, it was always better to harm a stranger than someone you knew.

"Bao Meng'er was never a saint," I told the officers. "But he was never the depressed type, either. In fact, given the chance, he would probably use one of his sons as a shield to block a bullet. Such is his nature."

After the skinny cop finished writing the word "nature," he exited the cruiser and let me out. I saw Mishu standing by the window, blowing on it and then writing Xs. Bao sat in a wheelchair next to her, and when he noticed me looking at him, he raised his arm and gave me a thumbs up.

Bao Meng'er stayed in the hospital for three months. Mishu slept on the bed next to her husband's when it was empty, and moved to a chair when it was occupied. One day, I brought them a pot of boiled eggs and a liter of hawthorn juice and found her napping at the foot of Bao Meng'er's bed like a curled-up cat. Mr. Jiang was forced to pay the hospital expenses. In addition, he sent Bao Meng'er a check for twenty thousand *yuan* to cover what the police had called "irreparable occupation damage." Bao was still classified as a poor peasant, a farmer—the use of his legs "integral" to his work—even though I hadn't seen him pick up a spade in years.

After leaving the hospital, he rented an apartment outside Xinchun Village, on the third floor of a newly constructed suite where the coal miners lived. His sons often visited him, even those living in the city who had, before his accident, only came home during the Spring Festival. During the few times he returned to Xinchun—to soak with his friends in the perfumed waters of Tang Ming Baths, to purchase meat from his favorite butcher, or to buy herbal medicine from Old Wisdom—villagers observed that he had grown wise with age, even generous with his tips. Old Wisdom claimed that Bao Meng'er had told him, after complaining about pain in his lower back, that we old people needed to learn from the young, to embrace life to the fullest and not worry so much about death. "Pain," Bao told Old Wisdom, "is like experience: both are veils that distort life's truths."

By chance, on one of my trips to the city to sell off extra tomatoes, I came across Mr. Jiang again. He was in a bad shape, begging next to a bus stop. He wore the same clothes as the last time I'd seen him. It was only after I dropped a ten-*yuan* bill into his pail that he looked up. It took him a second to recognize me.

"Where's your van?" I asked, understanding that it was a stupid question as soon as I said it.

"Confiscated by the state," he said. "Driving without a license. They didn't even let me sell it." His mother, he told me, passed away a week ago. None of his friends had money, so in order to avoid jail, he had to borrow from a couple of loan sharks. He wasn't able to repay his debts on time, and they took away his wife and daughter as collateral. They told him they'd only make the two of them do honest labor—wash dishes, scrub laundry, polish nails—but who could be sure they'd keep their word?

"Where are the police now?" he asked me. "Where are the police now?"

I told him he should try and get them out somehow, that they should come to our village and hide out. "We don't have much," I said, "but at the very least, I could offer all of you three meals a day and a warm bed. Given your situation, I'm sure my daughter-in-law won't mind."

He shook his head and pushed me aside.

"Please." I reached into my pocket for some cash. "Here. This is half of what I earned today. I'll give you my son's phone number if you just wait a while longer for me to remember."

He grabbed the money. "Go away," he said. "You're blocking my view of the people getting off the buses."

I came home feeling exhausted. I went to our bedroom and lay down, turning my head so that I could see my family doing work in our center yard. My wife and daughter-in-law chopped vegetables while my son counted the money I had made that day.

"Taking your afternoon nap?" my wife called.

I didn't respond. *Were these people my family?* I asked myself. I'd fall asleep, I knew, and wake up to a cold, lonely dinner.

WHERE CLOUDS RAIN PEARLS

On Thursday, before my Uncle Wen from the United States was supposed to arrive, I took the bus to downtown Yuncheng to rent a Cadillac. My uncle's train from Beijing, where he had flown for business, was arriving around noon, so I had to wake up at seven-thirty, four hours earlier than usual. On the bus, I sat next to a peasant woman with her two boys. The woman carried a dirty straw bag and wore tattered pants that didn't extend beyond her ankles. The bus wasn't heated, and her boys, both around ten, had the same oversized scarf wrapped around their shoulders. The three of them stank like rotten leeks. I didn't notice the smell until it was gone, half an hour later, when they got off at Xinchun, a local village where my Uncle Jin still lived with my grandma.

A man named Fa owned the car dealership. My family had rented cars from him in the past, for big occasions like my aunt's wedding or my grandfather's funeral. Still, the old split-lipped man tried to pass one over on me. I asked him for their newest Cadillac, and he tried to add a depreciation fee.

"What do you think you're doing?" I said. I opened the car door and smelled the leather. "This doesn't even smell new. It smells like wax."

"People who don't drive quality cars don't know what real leather smells like. The price per day is five hundred, plus one hundred for the fee."

"My parents only gave me three hundred."

He ran his thumb down the slit of his lip several times before answering. "Because I know your parents well, I'll rent you the car. Just know I'm doing this to save them face."

The car was called a Cadillac Sedan and it was better than anything I'd ever driven. It was black with four doors, power windows, and a sunroof. I had gotten my license a while ago, after convincing my dad to bribe an automotive clerk in Yuncheng. Since then, I'd only driven my friend's moped. My parents had promised to borrow some money and buy me a car after I'd graduated from Shanxi University, but since I'd never graduated, they never had to. I'd been out of college for close to six months now. A part of my father had probably been glad that I'd never graduated, though he'd never been the type to keep a promise.

On my way back from the city, I drove past the same bus I came on. Seeing those poor peasants on the bus watching me, I lowered the sunroof and blasted the pop song playing on the radio. It was freezing out, being mid-November, but I sped past the bus, almost hitting a three-wheeled taxi in front of me. Giddy, I breathed in the cold and smelled smoke from the local coal refinery, the aroma like roast duck. I thought of my uncle coming from America and keeping my parents busy so they'd lay off my case for the next few days, and I thought of the two hundred *yuan* left over in my pocket, and life started to taste as sweet as a dozen date cakes during the Lunar Festival.

I drove directly to the train station. All my family was there, waiting for Uncle Wen to arrive. Uncle Jin was buying a lamb kabob from a street vendor for his daughter—my cousin, Lan—and my mother was combing Lan's hair with a brush so big that it looked like it was made for horses. My dad sat next to them on a green bench, not hearing me pull up.

Uncle Jin was the loser of my grandma's three children. He still lived with my grandma in the village, in the same house he had grown up in, planting government-subsidized wheat and sorghum and bringing the leftovers to sell in Yuncheng City. Uncle Wen had graduated from Beijing University and left for New York to get a PhD in microbiology. In terms of success, my father was somewhere in between. He had left the village when he was twenty-five to fight in the Vietnam War. When he returned, he borrowed money from his brother in America and started a supermarket on the outskirts of Yuncheng, in a once prosperous part of the city that was now slowly becoming a landfill. We lived upstairs of the supermarket, in clear view of watermelon peels, plastic bags, spoiled rice, and dog feces.

My cousin Lan saw me get out of the car and ran over to give me a hug. She was six years my junior, turning seventeen this December, and we'd become close ever since I'd left college and started borrowing my friend's moped to take her out to sing karaoke. Sick of the countryside, she was determined to marry a man from the city, preferably one graduating from Shanxi University. Skinny and short, she looked best in rural clothes, in dotted blouses and clay-striped pants. I introduced her to a few of my friends, and when we went out to bars or pool halls, I made sure none of them took advantage of her.

"Older brother," she said. "When are you taking me to meet more of your friends?" Today she was wearing a short, checkered skirt and her hair, straight and full, ran down her back as if it were all one wide strand. She jumped up and down to keep warm, nibbling on the kabob.

"You must be freezing." I took off my leather jacket—imitation leather—and wrapped it around her shoulders. "How did you convince Grandma to let you wear that in this temperature?"

"Grandma didn't object," Lan said. "She wanted me to look good for Uncle Wen."

"You look like a prostitute," I said. "Only poor uneducated farmers find prostitutes attractive. Grandma doesn't know anything."

"I know," she said, pulling a chunk of lamb from the skewer. Her lips were becoming blackened from the meat. "That's why you need to take me shopping. You need to show me what college girls wear."

I took out a cigarette and lit it between closed palms. I'd smoke whenever I'd see something pathetic in my family, and sometimes, despite my best efforts, I found it hard to separate Lan from all the other peasant girls in my grandma's village.

"Let me have one," she said.

"Are you stupid?" I swatted her hand away. "Uncle Jin and Grandma are right there."

She gave me a nagging cry, the type she'd give her parents or Grandma whenever she didn't get what she wanted. It was a sound I often heard made by the girls I knew, an extended and high-pitched *na* that slowly faded away. They made these noises because they were used to getting what they wanted: the only child in a country where girls were few.

The girl I'd been engaged to in college, Qian, made a similar noise whenever she ate something she didn't like. We fought constantly because I was also used to getting what I wanted. We were together for a year and I wanted out of the relationship, but her parents were the ones who paid for my tuition, all forty thousand *yuan* of it. Her parents were party members, her father the assistant mayor of Yuncheng, and they saw me as an investment in their daughter's future.

"You want to see the inside of a Cadillac?" I opened the door and motioned for Lan to get in. She handed me the skewer, smoothed her skirt as she sat down, and turned the steering wheel with greasy fingers, bouncing in the seat.

I took another drag of my cigarette, exhaled above the car's hood, and saw my dad making his way over. The wind blew up his combover. He re-parted it and held it down with two fingers. I knew what he was going to ask.

"How much you pay for the rental?"

"Fa's a stingy old egg," I said. "Charged us extra. Added a depreciation fee." I spat on the ground for emphasis. I was so good at lying to my father that he thought I was a moron when it came to bargaining.

"You didn't even try," he said. "Your generation doesn't think about money." He looked at Lan inside the car and then back at me, and gave me a disgusted wave as he walked off and rejoined my mom and Uncle Jin.

I didn't protest when my dad had first mentioned the idea of getting the Cadillac. But I wasn't sure what he was trying to prove. Uncle Wen would know the car didn't belong to us once he saw our house and the piles of garbage a few meters in front of our door. Five hundred *yuan* to save a half hour's worth of face didn't seem like a good deal to me.

The train came in fast, like it wasn't going to stop. I took a step back from the rail and felt the air blowing against my face. After a couple of compartments had passed, the brakes squeaked and the train stopped. When Uncle Wen stepped off, the first thing I noticed about him was how young he looked. My father was the oldest of my grandfather's three children, and Uncle Jin was the youngest, about eight years younger than Uncle Wen, but already Jin's skin was dry and wrinkled from working in the fields and his front teeth were chipped from chewing on coarse rice. Uncle Wen, by contrast, had a full head of black hair and hands like a calligrapher's. He carried a small suitcase that had large wheels and an extendable handle.

I drove the car. In the back, Uncle Wen sat between my father and Uncle Jin, and up front, Lan sat between me and my mom. My mom was telling Lan how pretty she'd gotten, asking her if she was ready to get married. I tried to drown out their chatter, glancing back at Wen and my father. Wen was saying how they really shouldn't have spent the money renting such an expensive car, how he didn't even drive a car this good in the United States. "Don't be silly," my father said. "Didn't you tell us you own four cars in America?" "Yes," Wen said, "but they're used. Their total value doesn't add up to this one." They got to the topic of my future, and Wen told my father that he'd be able to get me into an American college if I did well on my TOEFL entrance exam. "What do you think about your uncle's offer, Yu?" my father called to me. I glanced at him in the rearview mirror but didn't say anything. "The boy will never amount to much," he finally said to my uncle. "He's lazy. Doesn't get up until noon." Bastard, I thought. I knew he was still bitter about the cost of the Cadillac. Uncle Jin kept his mouth shut the entire trip, embarrassed, I suspected, sitting next to his two successful brothers.

By the time we reached the house, I wanted to get the hell out of there and start drinking at the karaoke bar. Uncle Wen told me to study hard for the exam, and he'd see what he could do about getting me into America. What else could I do but lie and smile and nod as if I believed I had any potential at all?

Wen didn't say anything about the garbage in front of our house, but as we made our way into the living room, he lifted his shiny black shoes and peeled off a sticky piece of cardboard. He inspected our supermarket aisle by aisle, picking up jars of tofu, dried shrimp skin, and pickled cabbage. He gave my father a nondescript nod, leaving for us to determine whether it was one of approval or disdain. "You've done well," he said when we reached the parlor. "I'm glad my investments were put to good use." My father smiled, his face reddening.

I was ashamed for my father. I had seen this man only once in my life before, when I was very young, before grade school, and though I respected him for his achievements, I didn't like the way my father cowered in front of him, didn't like the way this man was judging us. I took a packet of dried dates from the supermarket and began eating while they talked, spitting the seeds not far from where Uncle Wen sat.

"All of you to the kitchen!" my father said. He motioned for me, my mom, and Lan to leave. "The men are discussing serious matters!" Uncle Jin started getting up too but sat back down when he heard the word "men."

I tapped Lan on the shoulder. She was fidgeting with her nails, trying to get the dirt out of them. Then I realized something was wrong with her. I figured she was sad because Uncle Wen never bothered talking to her about taking the TOEFL entrance exam. "You want to go somewhere?" I whispered.

"Sure." She looked up, beaming.

We slipped out from the back and I took out the Cadillac keys, feeling the two hundred *yuan* bills sweaty in my pocket. Lan followed, standing on her tiptoes to avoid contact with the garbage. "Older brother," she asked, "where're we going?"

"Anywhere you'd like, Lan. Your older brother has money tonight."

We got into the Cadillac, and instantly—just like that—the world changed. There was an air freshener hanging from the rearview mirror and the car smelled like pine trees. I hadn't even realized how foul the air by our house was. Being around garbage so much, you tend to get used to everything foul.

I'd known Qian, the girl I thought I'd marry, since before college. We'd gone to the same high school together, a private school in downtown Yuncheng my father could only afford after receiving money from Uncle Wen. I failed most of my classes and graduated only because, by twelfth grade, Qian and I were a couple, and the principal knew that Qian's father was a big shot Party member.

Qian had been a shy girl when I'd first known her, a good student who sat up front and copied her lessons and understood math. I sat in the back and watched her. One day, the teacher had us recite a lesson on the Three Warring States, and when I couldn't, she paired us up so that Qian could tutor me. In the middle of our first lesson, I got up and lit a cigarette. She asked if I was afraid of getting cancer, and I asked why she cared. It was a line I had often used with other girls before, but Qian fell for it. Eventually, I got her to have dinner with me, and on our first date—at a KFC in Yuncheng's red-light district, where we heard men picking up prostitutes outside—I took her hair into my hand and told her that one strand of it was worth more than my life.

A month later, by the city limits, atop one of the remaining sections of Yuncheng's city walls, built during the Ming Dynasty, we had sex for the first time. I didn't admit that it was my first time, too, virginity at odds with the cynical persona I tried to create. We were lying together in the dark and we heard an old knife-sharpener yelling in the streets to come get your knife or scissors sharpened. Qian sneezed because of the dust near our noses and the knife sharpener's cart suddenly stopped. Afraid that he'd become the victim of thieves, he yelled, "Who's there?" I hooted like I was the ghost of his ancestor, and we heard him pushing his cart in a frightened half-trot down the street. Qian and I laughed for a long time. Later that night, thinking that it was my responsibility, I asked her to marry me.

By the time our relationship was over, Qian wasn't shy anymore. In college, she was like a caterpillar turning into a moth, and I was her cocoon. Leaving her home and meeting new people, she became acutely aware of her family's status, of what she was able to get out of life that others couldn't. She planned out our future: I was studying economics because she wanted me to be a businessman. After graduation, we were to move to Beijing or Shanghai and start a family. "You're so good with people, Yu," she told me. "And with my father's connections, you'll be very successful." I wasn't sure what I was thinking at the time, because from as far back as I could remember I had never minded a handout, but right then I saw the rest of my life being controlled by this spoiled girl and her family, unsatisfied with myself because everything I'd have would be because of someone else.

I didn't have the heart or courage to call the wedding off, but I didn't care much about the relationship anymore. One day I wanted to go out drinking but Qian wanted to stay in and study for an exam. I told her that we could study for it tomorrow, that I did my best work cramming the night before. She laughed. "The only reason," she told me, "that you got into college was because of my father. The only reason you're still here is because of him." Before that moment

I'd always tried to shrug off those remarks. But in hindsight, they were like droplets of water filling up a dinghy, and at that moment, I was filled to the brim, ready to sink. I never forgot the look of indignation on her face after I hit her: her hand on her cheek; her eyes thin and narrow, staring at me like two black pebbles.

She called her parents; the wedding was off. When I failed my next class at Shanxi University, I bought a ticket home to Yuncheng. On the train ride back, I passed sorghum and leek fields like the one my father had grown up on. It was winter, the windows foggy from the number of passengers on the train. I wiped off the steam with my palm. I remembered a time in my childhood when the supermarket hadn't been making too much money, and my father told my mother that if times got even worse, they could always move back to the village, to my grandfather's land, where they'd always have a place to fall back on. His words, instead of comforting my mother, made her cry. I remembered thinking then that I'd rather commit suicide than live with Uncle Jin and Grandma.

The owners of the new karaoke bar—Man-ha-ton's—bragged that it used bricks shipped over from New York for its construction. There was a white bartender, maybe American but most likely Russian, who had a translator whispering customers' orders into his ear.

When we got there, my friend Jiang and his friend were sitting by the entrance, waiting for a room to open up. He told me that he saw Qian the other day, singing with this guy he didn't know. I looked into each room as we passed, examining faces under disco balls, but she wasn't there. We ended up renting a room with Jiang and his friend Liu, next to rooms that hosted a double date and a bachelor party. I sat between Lan and my friends because I thought her skirt exposed too much thigh.

"What are we drinking?" Jiang asked. Then, before I could answer, he looked over my shoulder and asked Lan. "What do you want to drink, little girl?"

"Drinks are on me." I stood up to make a toast. "My successful uncle has returned from America. He has returned from where streets are paved with platinum, where soda flows from faucets, and where clouds rain pearls. He has given me a taste of the bounty." I took out the two hundred *yuan* and held them up to the light. Then with a broad sweep of my arm I slapped them down onto the table. "So tonight, for his honor, we drink Budweiser."

Jiang and Liu laughed, raising invisible glasses to make me an invisible toast. Lan looked at them and raised her arm as well, timidly, her hand in a fist.

After the first beer, to get the mood going, Jiang, Liu, and I took turns singing songs like *Xing Qiu Ra Ke*, "Alien Planet Rock," *Bu Da Bu Xiao*, "Not Big, Not Small," and *Wo De Huang He Niu Zi*, "My Yellow River Girl." For the first few songs, despite Jiang and Liu's best efforts to get Lan to sing, she just sat there and sipped on her beer, holding the neck of the bottle with both her hands. But after two or three beers, Jiang got Lan to sing "A Whole New World" with him. He lifted and dipped his arm during the carpet ride sequence, and pressed his hand against his chest, cocking his head sideways, during the line "Don't you dare close your eyes." Lan had never seen the movie, and she couldn't read very well, so she filled in the words she didn't know with what she thought they should be. We were all getting tipsy, and I heard Jiang's friend Liu laughing each time Lan made a mistake. By her fifth Budweiser, she was the only one up there singing. She was drunk, and she flipped through the selection binder to find the songs she wanted to sing. I lit a cigarette and tried to ignore Jiang and Liu laughing next to me.

"Who knew?" Jiang said. He nodded his head towards Lan, who

was singing in front of the TV, oblivious of the world, jumping up and down.

"What?" I said.

"Who knew your cousin could sing well?" There was a drunken haze in his eyes.

"Who knew," I repeated. I gave him a look that told him if he went any further I'd give him something serious to feel for the rest of the night.

He didn't seem to notice. "Hey country princess," he yelled. "Why don't you sing the swallow song for us?"

We all knew the swallow song, knew it since we were kids: *Little swallow, wearing a white coat, every year, you come here. I ask you, Why do you come? And you say, The springs here are the most beautiful.* We all sang it as kids, and it was a country song, and I didn't think it was appropriate for Lan to sing in a karaoke bar.

She was flipping through the binder, though, looking for the song, taking sips of her Budweiser, when I got up and said we had to go.

"So soon? I just found it in the book."

I lifted her up by the arm and told her she was drunk.

"So soon?" Jiang mimicked Lan's voice, sending Liu into an uproar.

I swung my coat around her shoulders and pulled her out of the room as she was trying to wave the two men goodbye.

We were silent in the car. I had the feeling Lan was waiting for an explanation, but I didn't feel like saying anything. I was protecting her, and I didn't owe her an apology.

"What's wrong with you?" she finally said. "I was having a good time."

"You don't want to be with those guys." I kept my eyes on the road.

"I thought they were nice enough."

"They were making fun of you."

"So what?" she said. "I'm used to it. It's not like I'm going to find a guy from the city who *isn't* going to make fun of me."

"Then stop trying to find a guy from the city," I said, turning up the radio. "Marry someone from the village. Stop humiliating yourself."

"You're one to talk about humiliation," she said. "You were going to marry that girl—what's her name—because her father was wealthy. You were like her dog, doing whatever she told you to."

I forgave her words because I knew she was drunk, and also because I was a little drunk, but at any other time I might have hit her. "Well," I said, "we didn't end up marrying, did we? I stuck up for myself, found whatever little pride I still had left, something that you should've done with those guys at the bar back there."

Lan was resting her head against the window, fogging it up with her breath. She wrote one word on the glass: *fuqi*—arrogance. "Why didn't you marry her?" she said, and then, when I didn't say anything, she added, "You should've married her."

"And why's that?"

"Because then we'd be related."

I laughed, but I knew what she meant. "Don't be silly. We're already related."

"No," she said. She looked at me then, believing that I had really misunderstood her. "I meant me and *her* would be related."

When I pulled up next to the garbage lining my street, it was close to midnight and Lan had already fallen asleep. Being a farmer, she was used to going to bed early and getting up before sunrise, something that I'd always admired about her.

Parked in front of me was a strange vehicle, a car that was even better than the one I was in. A black BMW, it reflected moonlight from its roof and door handle, and it took me a second to realize that it belonged to Qian's family. I looked around and saw the driver standing in front of my house, eating a steamed bun with Uncle Jin, who waved when he saw me staring at him. He ran over and I rolled down the window.

"She's been inside for almost an hour waiting for you," Jin said. He peered over the steering wheel at Lan, who was passed out with her head on my shoulder. He smiled. "Fun night?" he asked. "Lan always loved going to the city. Too bad she doesn't like going to the city with me anymore. She says I embarrass her. When she was eight or nine years old, when I went to Yuncheng in the summertime to sell dried apricots, I couldn't shake her off."

I shook Lan's shoulder, trying to wake her.

"Don't bother," Jin said. "I like seeing her this way. You go in there and take care of your business. I'll see to it that she gets to bed."

When I opened the door to my family's yard, I saw Qian sitting under the dim yellow light. Our family's bench was next to the kitchen and it didn't have a backrest, but Qian was sitting up straight. She wore a pair of glasses I'd never seen before and a coat with two sets of buttons and she carried a small purse that dangled down to her knees. She got up and looked through the open door, past me, to where Uncle Jin was helping Lan out of the Cadillac. She looked at me, then at Lan, and then back at me again.

"I'm not here to see you," she said. "My parents heard about your uncle coming and I'm here to see him. You should know that none of this was my idea. My parents made me come. I'm doing this for them."

My uncle was carrying Lan around his shoulder. He pushed

the front door as wide as possible and smiled apologetically as he passed us. "Quickly!" Lan said. "Can we go a little faster? It's freezing out here."

After they left, I tried to explain. "We're not what you think we are," I said. " It's funny that you would even think that."

"There's no need to explain," Qian interrupted. "As I said before, I'm not here for you; I'm here for your uncle. But it *is* good to see you again, Yu. It's good to see that you still take yourself seriously. And I'm happy you found someone just like you to be with."

She turned around and started walking to the living room. She opened the door and shook Uncle Wen's hand. Before closing the door, Uncle Wen looked at me curiously, as if waiting for me to explain the situation. I saw my mother and father sitting behind him. They probably had known as soon as Qian was at the door what this was going to be about, and I wasn't surprised that they still hadn't told him.

Standing outside, I could hear what Qian was saying to my uncle: "Fact of the matter is your family owes my family forty thousand *yuan*, and at least in my family, debts are settled whenever it becomes possible to settle them." I peered into the glass window on the door and saw my father glaring back at me. Uncle Wen was sitting still with his legs crossed. Every once in a while he raised a jar of tea and sipped from it. Qian was sitting on the arm of a couch. I was seeing her side profile and she was sitting very straight, both her hands over her purse on her lap.

Uncle Jin returned from the bedroom a few minutes later with a bun in his mouth and several stuffed buns wrapped in toilet paper in his hands. I shook my head, breathed in through my nose to make him think the water in my eyes was because of the cold.

"They're pork and leek," he said. "Take it. You grandma was up all night making them. We only eat food this good twice, maybe three times a year."

I took a bun and started taking big heavy bites. When I was nine or ten, every year I looked forward to the Spring Festival to eat shrimp peel dumplings and rice noodles and steamed leek buns. Feeling the texture of the bun against my cheeks and the leek and pork spilling onto my tongue, I tried putting myself back in that time again, when food had been the most important thing for me and my family.

"Things seem to be serious in there," Jin said. He took a bun and began eating it slowly, closing his eyes and trying to picture the taste.

I nodded.

"Don't be afraid," he said. "Uncle Wen won't let anybody take advantage of the family."

I nodded again and rubbed my greasy hands on my fake leather jacket.

"He's got a trump card, you know. He's the last tile on the mah-jong table, as powerful as Chairman Mao himself. That girl in there: she's never been to the places your uncle has been. Her father's connections pale to Uncle Wen's. Uncle Wen—he is family. Your interests are his interests. Him, me, your father—we're brothers." He hit his chest twice with a closed fist. "It only takes one of us for the three to succeed."

I offered him a cigarette and took one for myself. We turned around and looked into the window on the door. Uncle Wen was now the one talking. We watched my uncle talk, watched him speak to Qian in a dismissive manner. He was standing up now and telling the girl that assumptions made about other people's income were never a good idea, that America was not what she thought it was and that her coming here tonight wasn't going to change the fact that he didn't have the money and that her parents had made a poor investment.

I stood there with Jin and could tell that Qian, like the rest of us, didn't believe a word my uncle was saying. I knew she didn't care either way. This wasn't what she wanted; this was what her parents had told her to do, one of her many duties separating her from where she wanted to be and what she wanted to do. I could tell that the way my uncle was talking to her now bothered her. She'd probably never had anyone talk to her in this manner her entire life. My uncle didn't even bother putting down his tea. He held the jar with both hands, one on the handle and the other on the bottom, talking to Qian in the way he had talked to my dad. He had the same expression on his face as when we had first picked him up in the Cadillac: unimpressed. He didn't care if the girl drove a BMW or that her family was powerful in Yuncheng. For Lan, my parents, and me, Qian's life was something to aspire to: we were country folk looking up at city folk as if they were bright unreachable stars. But to Uncle Wen, we were all the same. The very reason that she was there talking to him, asking him for money, put her in the same category as the rest of us. To Uncle Wen, Qian and my father were both under the same umbrella of pathetic-ness that he was here to deal with.

After Qian came out, I didn't even bother telling her that Lan was my cousin. She left our yard, her purse dangling from her hand, tiptoeing around the garbage to where her driver stood with the car door open.

I walked back inside. Uncle Wen was reading a book under a lamp as if nothing had happened. My mom and Uncle Jin were wiping off the table, storing the buns in a cool dry basket to save for the morning.

My dad was standing by my bedroom door, waiting for me. He didn't say anything about Qian. He asked me if I knew what I had to do in the morning. He didn't care anymore whether or not Uncle Wen heard. "Don't want to get charged for another day," he said. "Make sure you wake up early." I put my hand in my pocket, touched the keys, and told him that I'd try.

AT THIS MOMENT, IN THIS SPACE

Paul Hwang does not have any more sons. Just a year ago, he had three, but now he doesn't have any. Long ago, he had chosen their American names: Jeremy, Michael, John, and Paul. (He never had a fourth son, and when he became a US citizen at the age of forty-six, he decided to take the final name as his own.) A missionary, Jeff, had traveled to Paul's village when he was ten and the villagers allowed the westerner to give English names to the four boys born during his visit. The tiny Chinese village had never seen a mission-ary before, though it'd heard of Christianity—*Tian Zhu Jiao*, or the faith of heaven's lord. Confused by the wording, Paul, like the oth-ers, interpreted *Tian Zhu Jiao* to be the religion that the gods them-selves worshipped. When he came to the United States, he thought of no better English names than the ones chosen by the missionary, this emissary for the gods' god.

But Paul isn't religious, or tries not to be. He knows that others are, and by naming his sons these names, he hoped they'd be able to fit in more easily with Americans. He also believed that, by chance if there was a God, God would be more inclined to forgive his unbelieving by the fact that he'd named his sons after the advice of the missionary. Paul is a superstitious man, though he'd be the last person to admit it, and he sees the recent turn of events—the death of his wife and two sons (the younger ones, Michael and John)—as somehow related, in the way that bad luck likes to chain, and also somehow his fault, in the way that his family would always gang up and blame him for everything when they had been alive.

A month ago, Paul's wife, Linda, and his two sons died in a car accident, hitting a pothole and ramming into a semi. Technically, Paul does have one son remaining, but they have not spoken in over six months. Jeremy is a junior at Yale, and a year ago he told Paul that he was switching majors from biology to history. Paul asked his son why, and the boy had the nerve to say that it was because he enjoyed it.

Paul is aware of the type of father he is, the type to admire his children from a distance, spinning futures for them. He always pictured Jeremy in a white coat, a stethoscope around his neck, parading down the cardiovascular wing of a hospital, the youngest heart surgeon in the state, like the curly-haired boy on that American TV show they had watched together as a family, *Doogie Howser, M.D.* This dream shattered, Paul resorted to ignoring his son, hoping vaguely that Jeremy would call him, apologize, and tell him that he was returning to his biology studies.

Before her death, his wife had snuck phone calls to Jeremy every month at work, and on occasion, Jeremy did the same. Paul's feelings about this were mixed. On one hand, Linda told him what was going on in Jeremy's life: the new girlfriend he had, the courses he was taking, the record of his ultimate Frisbee team. On the other hand, he resented the fact that his sole link to his eldest son was through his wife, who told him of Jeremy's affairs in a voice that suggested she had always been the closer parent.

Though Paul knows that it is his responsibility to tell his son of his mother's and brothers' deaths, he is too afraid to do so. Every day he stares at the cell phone, his hands shaking when he flips through the address book to find his son's name highlighted and glowing.

Secretly, he hopes that Jeremy will find out on his own. This is what he envisions: After a month of not hearing his mother's voice, Jeremy calls her company. When he asks for Linda Hwang, the person on the other end, the receptionist, will remain silent for a few seconds. She considers whether or not to ask who is calling. To distance herself, she decides she'd better not, and she tells the young man in a hushed voice that she is sorry, but Linda Hwang has passed away. Finally, as a way of closing the conversation, she asks whether he'd like the phone number of the family.

Paul plays this scene again and again in his head, but he can never picture his son's reaction. Would he be angry and disbelieving, or sad and resigned? Would he demand to speak to her boss, the CEO of the small pharmaceutical where Linda worked? Would he hang up, opting to call home right away? Or would he be too scared, like his father, too scared to even call at all?

When Paul thinks about these possible outcomes, he feels that he no longer knows his son. So much has changed since Jeremy left for college. He'd been timid in high school, a boy terrorized by rejection. He played video games and ran track, the only sport that everyone got in. But the voice that Paul heard a few months ago, telling him that his son was not going to become a doctor, did not seem to belong to the same son that Paul remembered. It was a confident, uncompromising voice, one that knew what it wanted but not what was good for it.

These days, sitting alone at the dinner table waiting for the pressure cooker to finish steaming rice, Paul finds his mind repeating, like a looping answering machine, the same questions: Where has my son gone? Where have all my sons gone?

At the funeral, everyone asks about Jeremy. Paul is sipping black tea and breathing in the incense sticks burned for Linda, Michael, and John. A thin smoke rises from the skeletal wood and dissolves in the air in front of the framed picture. The picture was taken three years ago at Washington DC, the summer before Jeremy left for college, the Lincoln Memorial lurking in the background. Paul remembers taking the picture—he remembers being too scared to ask in his broken English for a passerby to take it for him. Jeremy is also in it, and the incense floating in front of the picture makes it seem as if he was also dead. Most of the people who are at the house know better, but Michael and John's piano teacher, Mrs. Ling, tells Paul how sorry she is about Linda and his three sons. Paul doesn't bother correcting her, the misunderstanding as much his fault as her own.

To closer friends, Paul's answer for Jeremy's absence is simple: It was *his* choice to not show up. "Still," headmaster Zhang from Chinese school, where Paul waited in front of a gym every Friday night so his sons could learn Mandarin, tells him, "It's Jeremy's duty. He should be here with you no matter what." This has the opposite effect of what the headmaster intends, since it also reminds Paul of his own duty to inform his son of his mother's and brothers' deaths.

Even Jeremy's friends from high school, the ones still stuck in Flushing, attending Hunter College or Nassau Community, disapprove of Jeremy's behavior. "I know Jeremy," Anthony Tai says, "He's just scared. It's not that he doesn't care about his mother or his brothers or you. He just doesn't want to or doesn't know how to deal with it. Can you blame him? Shit, if this happened to me,

I might do the same." This, too, does not comfort Paul. How dare this boy compare himself to Jeremy? Jeremy, who's attending Yale, and this kid, who's attending community college. "But I'll give him a call," Tai says, "to tell him how much of a wimp he's being." Paul considers this for a moment, going over the pros and cons of his son finding out in this manner, and then, in stern Chinese, he says, "No, you will do no such thing." The kid shrugs, turning around and making his way in his baggy black jeans over to the refreshments table.

Paul seems to be moving back in time. Each morning when he goes downstairs, his expectation of seeing his family grows. He seems to hear the two TVs—one of cartoons or sitcoms or pro-wrestling that Michael and John liked to watch, and the other of Chinese channels they receive over satellite that Linda enjoyed. He seems to smell scallion cakes frying in sesame oil, or the steam from Linda's rice and sweet potato porridge drifting up the stairs. These things were what he looked forward to when he woke up in the morning. Afterwards, he would drive for thirty minutes to Fordham University, where he teaches several sections of introductory physics and directs the graduate students in his lab, where long ago he gave up the hope of discovering anything of remote importance to humanity.

These mornings, Paul drives to work and thinks about theoretical physics. In the past, he did not believe in string theory. Until recently, theoretical physics has only been a bane to his existence. Funding for physical chemistry, his field, was cut to make room for a new particle accelerator, and he viewed this reallocation of resources as proof of the new decadence in academia: People were no longer interested in doing research on subjects that provided tangible results for the public. Instead, they wanted to shoot expensive protons and neutrons at a high speed and record the results, which could never increase crop yields or make the lives of factory workers less taxing. Once, he had told his peers about his views, and they had called him, jokingly, a communist.

Recently, though, Paul has been thinking seriously about M-theory, a part of string theory that deals with multiple dimensions. Every possible outcome exists on different planes of existence. To Paul, M-theory seems to suggest that there are an infinite number of dimensions where Linda and Michael and John are still alive. Better yet, there are an infinite number of dimensions where Linda and Michael and John are still alive *and* where Jeremy still talks to him. He remembers a conversation he had with his colleagues about recent developments in subatomic particles, about how certain antiparticles wink in and out of space-time. They come into our dimension briefly, and then vanish. No one knows where they go, but M-theory suggests that they might be entering into other dimensions. Dimensions, Paul considers, in which Linda and Michael and John might still be with him. Although these particles have only been discovered in atomic accelerators, Paul believes that, statistically speaking, there are particles on his body—or even parts of his own body—that are doing the same: winking in and out of existence. It comforts him to think that, however unlikely, this might be possible: that at this very moment he is exchanging particles with a world in which his family was still alive.

At work, his mind wanders, and he finds it difficult to concentrate on his experiments. He pours a liter of sulfuric acid up to the brim before realizing the beaker is too small. Acid spills over and begins eating away at the black tabletop. "*Ta ma de,*" he curses, and calls over a graduate student to douse the table with a strong base. "Don't worry, Dr. Hwang," the young man says. "This stuff happens all the time." He points to the other rings on the table. Paul feels an eroding pain in his thumb and palm, and he runs a weak base over his hand to numb it.

"Professor Hwang," he hears another student across the lab yell. He looks up and straightens his glasses with his thumb-knuckle. The student is holding out a phone, tiptoeing and waving to him. "Phone call," she says.

Suddenly he is filled with a rare kind of terror, one that he knew very well when he was a boy but seemed to have somehow forgotten. He is ten years old again, back in his village, and his parents had driven the mule-carriage that morning to sell leeks in the city. They left him instructions for what must be done in the fields, and now, at the end of the day, he remembers that he forgot to pull the weeds out of the cabbage area and to sprinkle the squash stands with pesticides. It's too late to start the work and his parents are going to be home any minute. He runs to the hut that Jeff the missionary calls a church. He hides there for the entire night. The American gives him cookies, and the sweetness of the chocolate chips makes him cry when he thinks about the beating his father will give him when he has to walk home in the morning.

He feels this fear again, now, at his lab where everyone around him is his subordinate. He takes the phone to his hand, and grasps it between his fingertips and the fat of his palm so that it doesn't come in contact with his thumb.

"Mr. Hwang," the voice says.

It is not Jeremy, and the elation leaves as quickly as it arrives: he will have to go through all of this again, and one of those times, it *will* be his son.

"I am Ted Franklin from Yale and I'm just calling to tell you that you've missed your last two payments. You still have plenty of time, but I do want to let you know that if we don't receive a payment from you by the end of this week, your son's registration for next semester might be delayed. We don't like to trouble the students with these types of things if we can resolve it with the parents first. The students are busy enough as it is with their schoolwork and social commitments. You understand."

"Can I pay over the phone?" Paul clears his throat, conscious of his accent. "I have my wallet with me now."

"Whatever is most convenient for you, Mr. Hwang."

Paul gives the man his credit card number, the expiration date, and the three-digit code. When the man hangs up, Paul combs his hand through his hair, the sweat on his fingertips trickling to the floor like glucose from an IV drip.

There is the spot where the accident happened. Nothing remains except for a ditch by the road, a section of scorched lawn no larger than a couple of square feet before the start of the woods. Paul drives past it every morning and afternoon. Each time he sees it he has the urge to turn around and go to The Home Depot, buy some lawn care product, drive back, and sprinkle seeds onto the seared patch. He'd like to just sit there and watch the patch grow until it looks like the surrounding grass. He doesn't do this because he is afraid of what incoming traffic might think. They would slow their SUVs and glance at him, wondering if his car broke down, and when they get close, they would realize that he is just a crazy Chinese man with nothing better to do than sit by the highway, with no knowledge of American etiquette.

And Paul thinks: they wouldn't be too far off. When he was young, he did not wear closed-up pants until the age of six. He wore pants with the bottoms cut open, like every other boy and girl in the village, for ease of defecation. There was no grass in China, Paul considers, not like the kind by the highway, so full and tall and green.

Villages couldn't afford to let such wasteful plants suck up nutrients from the wheat and sorghum fields, and children's defecation, however unpleasant it might be to look at or smell, enriched the soil. It was all about practicality, not beauty or ambience. He might not be familiar with American etiquette, but he bets most Americans couldn't even conceive of what it means to grow up in China, where the notion of labor isn't sitting behind a desk writing on paper or driving a truck that lifts the crates for you.

Paul thinks these thoughts and then questions where his resentment comes from. He doesn't want to feel this way about the country he lives in, the country his wife and sons died in, and the country his remaining son is getting his education in. In a perfect world—his belief in the existence of this perfect world growing with each day after their deaths—he would not feel resentment at what's been given to him, or sorrow for his loss, or fear of doing the simplest and most common of activities.

He has taken up meditation. Though he doesn't believe in Buddhism or Daoism or the benefits of yoga, he sits cross-legged and erect for hours at a time. The other day, he checked out some books at the library. Not bothering to read the words, he glanced through the pictures and diagrams and tried to contort his body to be the same as those shown on the page.

Now, he closes his eyes. He tries to not think at all but to feel beyond the atoms of his body. Is this the one winking into another dimension? What about this one at the tip of his toe? He wonders if the pin-like sensation he just felt is a particle from another universe. He wonders if he has just come into contact with another, luckier, version of himself.

Ridiculous, he thinks.

It is one of those days that Paul believes God does not have the power to make worse. There is no sun, the sky a smokestack gray that forces him to turn on the lights at lunchtime. The air is damp, and just as he enters the parking lot to drive home, it starts to drizzle. By the time he reaches the highway he has his wipers on full. To make matters worse, his accelerator doesn't work, and when he looks down to check the gas he sees that the engine temperature needle has shot up beyond the maximum. He pulls his car to the side of the highway, conscious of the annoyed vehicles behind him having to slow down and veer left. When he opens the hood, the radiator is smoking. The rain helps somewhat to cool it down, and after it becomes safe enough to touch, he pulls away some of the wires and sees that the coolant-feeding tube is cut and fluid is leaking. The nearest auto mechanic is fifteen miles away. He spends three hours getting there, driving for five minutes at a time, checking the temperature, pulling over, and then waiting for the engine to cool.

He is soaked when he gets home. There is a message on his answering machine, and at first he is too afraid to check it. He wants to hit erase, but he forces himself to press the button next to it, and he is relieved when he hears that it is Danny from the lab telling him that, before he left the office, he had forgotten to centrifuge several test tubes of a benzene solution.

The phone rings again as soon as he hits the erase button, and for a moment, Paul doesn't suspect it to be anyone else.

"Hello," he says.

There is a dropped breath, a sigh, and Paul knows who it is as soon as he hears it.

"Hi, Dad. I tried calling Mom's extension at work but it was disconnected." A pause, long enough to signify annoyance but not sadness. "To be honest," his son continues, "I was hoping that Mom would be the one to pick up instead of you. If she's there and you still don't want to talk to me, you can just put her on."

Of course, Linda's extension. Why would Jeremy bother going through the receptionist at all? Paul thinks for a moment, going over the excuses he has prepared over the last week to explain why he hasn't called him or told him of the accident and the funeral. He has not prepared for the possibility that his son might call and not know about the situation. None of his excuses make sense. "Your mom—" he says. "Your mom left a while ago."

"That's OK. I can talk to you about this, too."

Paul is silent. He knows that if he doesn't say anything now, there will be no other opportunity to correct his previous statement. But what about the funeral? What about the fact that he has denied his son of seeing his mother for the last time? Is a lie made during a phone call really so significant, he asks himself, when compared to what he has done already? He opens his mouth, but he is too late.

"It's simple, really. I got an e-mail from Yale accounting yesterday. They said you guys haven't been keeping up with payments. I can't register for next semester." His son's voice is expedient, efficient even, with the firm belief that the biggest problem in his life is whether or not he will be able to register for classes.

Paul feels a hint of betrayal from Yale, from—*What was his name?*—but it is gone after a second, and his mind begins to wander. He wonders if he is seeing the situation in the wrong way. After all, he thinks, isn't this what he has been hoping for all along?

"Dad," Jeremy says.

"I'm here."

"Is something wrong at home?"

For a moment, Paul is terrified again. His son is tricking him. He knows everything, and this is how he gets his vengeance. Paul can see him, on the other end of the phone, his face angry like the way his own father had been after he returned home with the chocolate chip cookie in his hand. For the next week, his father made him do double his chores, and whenever they went to the missionary's hut on Sundays, his father would turn and look at him as if he had dishonored the family in front of the entire village.

"Are you guys in some kind of financial problem? Did Mom get laid off? Tell me, Dad. I can get a part-time job or a work-study position. It's not hard."

He feels his body being pulled apart. Numbness surges through his hands, his feet, and his head. It's like his organs were placed in separate containers and then pressed so that blood could not enter any of them. He is no longer sure which world he is in.

"Dad. Talk to me. Should I get a temporary loan? If you can't get the money by this week, I'm going to have to do that. And really, it's no big deal at all."

This is a gift from God, Paul thinks. It is as if he has entered into another universe, one in which the biggest problem is paying for his son's tuition.

These must be it, these tingles.

Soon, perhaps in a few seconds, he will lose all memories that don't belong.

"You still there, Dad?"

"Yeah," Paul says. He is speaking English now, suddenly not conscious of his accent. "Don't worry, Jeremy. I've taken care of everything."

NEW WORK IN NEW CHINA

Young Huli has pushed back the remnants of the Communist Party to Inner Mongolia. His tanks and yellow-shirted infantry have crushed the guerrillas that controlled the provinces below the Yangtze River and the remaining People's Liberation Army militia along the Yellow River. He has declared himself emperor. His armies march across the provinces waving blue banners with yellow half-moons, the new symbol for China.

To celebrate his victories, the young emperor builds a palace in his homeland of Tibet that borders the Gobi Desert, the remnants of the Great Wall stretching in the background. To fill it, he has chosen one virgin from every province to be his concubine. This, he explains to the Chinese people, signifies the country's unification into greatness. And the girls, whom he will treat equally by going to bed with a different one every day of the month, represent his equal treatment of all the provinces. New China consists of thirty-one provinces, and he has declared that in the months when there are only thirty days, he will not sleep with Manchuria.

In order to appease the growing demand for democracy—mostly among college students—the emperor has given his concubines certain powers. They will act as a sort of sexual senate. Each concubine will act as a representative to her respective province. They will be able to propose laws, suggest amendments, encourage pardons, and ask the emperor for consideration as a judge or military commander, all on their scheduled nights when the emperor sleeps with them. The college students remain unsatisfied, but the emperor understands that one cannot force-feed democracy. Such sudden freedoms might burst the nation's stomach.

He believes his biggest problem will be keeping his palace court in order. Reforms bring about unforeseen obstacles: how will the emperor maintain control of his sexual senate? He decides to reinstate an old tradition used by the emperors of past dynasties: the recruiting and training of *gong-gongs*. A *gong-gong* is a manservant of the emperor and the emperor's concubines who, on appointment, is made a eunuch. The young emperor has read *Romance of the Three Kingdoms* and *Dreams of Red Mansion*, and he understands that in China's past, even when eunuchs and concubines were not given any *official* power, the public intrigue reached such levels that they were sometimes able to usurp the throne. He must pick his servants carefully.

One of the recent appointees is a man named Zhang Mei, a cook he met in Beijing during his siege of the city. The man is unusually loyal and trusting, but the emperor did not waive the cutting of the testicles. "Traditions," he said to Zhang Mei, who was kneeling before him. A tradition as important and as commonly known as the requirements to become a *gong-gong*, the emperor must strictly maintain.

Zhang Mei is not from the city. He was born in the countryside, and snuck into Beijing when he was twenty using a fake birth cer-

tificate. He did not know it was the new emperor Huli who was
enjoying his hand-drawn noodles during the Siege of the Beijing,
always sitting on that patch of dirt next to his concession stand. The
man's face looked more like a beggar's—covered with hair, his teeth
crooked, his nose long like an opium addict's pipe. He sat there and
ate and steam came out of his mouth, and he laughed with his entire
body when his soldiers said something funny. Zhang thought he
was an infantryman, or perhaps a tank commander. On one such
occasion, Zhang was standing in front of the strange man, pouring
him flour broth, when he saw a stray shrapnel flying toward them.
He knocked the hot shrapnel away with his wok. In the process,
he spilled the steaming broth on the soldiers. He was almost afraid
the hairy man would lob a grenade at his concession stand. Instead
the man thanked him and brought him to Tibet, then made him a
eunuch. Zhang Mei considers his current station in New China to
be most fortunate.

He has a cousin stuck in the countryside. This cousin, Pei Pei,
has recently married his village sweetheart, and their dream is to
live in Beijing or Shanghai. Zhang wants to help them. He calls his
cousin using his government-issued phone and urges him to come
to Tibet and work for the emperor.

"You won't have to worry about money anymore," Zhang says in
his new high-pitched voice. "Everyone will have to bow to you. I'll
put in a good word with the emperor."

At first Pei Pei thinks that the change in his cousin's voice is
due to the dry climate of the Gobi Desert. Then he realizes that it is
because his cousin is not a man anymore. Not having testicles, Pei
Pei realizes, affects you beyond your penis not hardening. Not only
is his cousin's voice not a man's anymore, it is not anything. Not
exactly a woman's voice. Not exactly a boy's squealing. It is bass-
less, like talking while being choked.

"Give me a few weeks, Zhang," he says. "Let me think about it."

"What's there to think?" Zhang says.

"Well, it's that Song and I want children."

"You can still have children. First put the bun in the furnace, then take the position."

"Will the emperor wait that long?"

"What do you mean?" Zhang says. "How hard can it be?"

"Well, we want more than one child. Do you think the emperor can wait a year or two?"

"I don't think so. He has already made many amendments regarding the appointment of *gong-gongs*. The emperor might start issuing an examination for it. This is an opportunity few people get. Think it over, Pei."

Pei Pei hangs up the phone. It is October and winter comes early in the countryside. He is sitting cross-legged in his mud shack, huddling on his stone bed in his sheepskin coat, smelling of urine. He turns around and looks at Song. She is squatting by the furnace, fanning the flames so she can begin to prepare dinner. She turns around, smiles, and says, "It's cold tonight. Dinner shouldn't be ready for a while." What will happen if they have children? He can see them, noses running, sitting around the fire with Song, waiting for their dinner, trails of flame flickering on their faces. She deserves better than this, he thinks.

The next morning Pei Pei goes to his parents' house to borrow some flour and hears his father talking on the phone. His father turns and smiles when he sees him coming in, and his mother gives him a large sack of flour, more than twice what she normally gives him.

"Brother Zhang tells me he can make you into a *gong-gong*," his father says. "Congratulations. Everyone here is very happy for you. Your mother and I are proud."

"What do you mean 'everyone'?" Pei Pei asks.

"Your brothers, sisters, uncles, aunts, everyone in the village," his mother says. "Do you expect us to keep news as good as this to ourselves?"

Pei Pei drops the sack of flour on the floor and covers his face. He sits down at his parents' table and becomes silent. He rests his elbows on his knees, his face still in his hands.

His father sits down next to him and pats his head. "You are young, Pei Pei," his father says. "I know you are at an age when your genitalia are very important to you. But it would be irresponsible of you not to take this position. You are the oldest in the family, and you have responsibilities. Brother Zhang tells me the emperor has allowed you to have children. You still have time to help Song conceive. As your father, and as an old man, I can tell you that genitalia are not as important in the future as you think. You have nothing to worry about. You will still be normal. Better than normal, in fact. Everyone will look up to you."

Pei Pei looks up. His face is covered with flour, white as death. He sniffles and then sneezes. Liquid drips out of his nose and eyes and streaks through the flour like rivers.

"Let me get you a towel," his mother says. She takes a dirty towel from the kitchen and wipes off his face.

He leaves his parents' house and walks home, the sack swung over his shoulder. On the way back, he notices the new way people look at him. They nod when he passes them, and smile, showing him teeth. He passes his old teacher. "Finally making something of yourself," the woman says. Pei Pei walks faster. He looks down and tries to hide his face, and when he gets home, he locks the door and barricades it with the sack.

"What's wrong?" Song says.

"You don't know? You haven't heard the news?"

"No," she says. "I've been cooking lunch." She stops fanning the furnace. "What's wrong?"

"Nothing," he says, calming down. "Everything is where it should be."

The emperor Huli knows that *gong-gongs* serve as much as they are served. He understands that those indentured to the powerful are also powerful themselves, that this is the way it has always been in imperial China. Because Zhang saved his life, the emperor has made him the head of his band of personal eunuchs. The emperor has read of a trend in *Romance of the Three Kingdoms* where eunuchs given to concubines aren't used as servants at all, but are played with like pets. The concubines dress them in female clothing and have them perform tricks and feed them treats. The emperor is careful not to put Zhang into this kind of humiliating situation. He respects Zhang's opinions and has given him a large mansion within the palace walls.

Inside his mansion, Zhang claps his hands twice. Two chambermaids enter the room carrying his cell phone and a pot of steaming water. They take off his clothes and scrub his body. He lifts the phone to his ear and calls his cousin.

"Just come for a visit," he tells Pei Pei. "Take a look at how extravagantly I am living."

"Give me some more time," Pei Pei says.

"I can't give you any more time," Zhang says. He stares at the chambermaids wiping off his body. They are wearing traditional Chinese dresses, pink with colorful jasmine designs, sashes folded over at the waist and then buckled with a black belt. He touches one of the girls' hair, and then reaches into her dress and feels her breast. He tries to remember what he felt like before he became a eunuch. He regrets not being able to do anything with her, but he manages to convince himself that he is in a better circumstance.

"If you're even considering this position," he says, "you need to come for a visit." The chambermaids put his clothes back on. "The emperor, and the concubine you're to be serving, want to see you. I can't convince them just by running my mouth."

He hangs up. He puts on his title hat, a black top hat with a topaz in the middle and two long rabbit-like ears protruding from the side, and opens the door. He swings his hand carelessly at the chambermaids and walks through the courtyard with his hands tucked behind his back. He passes peach trees and fountains and he forgets that it's winter and that he's in a desert. The entire courtyard is a greenhouse, under gigantic panels of glass.

He makes his way into the main palace. He walks past rolls of identical rooms until he comes to a red door with "Lady Jing" inscribed on it. Lady Jing is the newest concubine in the palace. The young emperor has recently returned from Henan province where he picked the sixteen-year-old Lady Jing from one of the poorest villages in the country. He told the people of Henan that he picked Lady Jing "because of her beauty, grace, and excellent acumen for law and justice."

The chambermaids lead Zhang into the interior, where the young girl is brushing her hair. Immediately, she turns around and smiles.

"I've been waiting for you all night!" she says.

"I had to make a call," Zhang says.

She stops brushing her hair, walks over to where Zhang is sitting, and starts playing with his title hat, flicking the rabbit ears back and forth. "There isn't one thing to do in this forsaken place!" she says.

"Not one *man* between fourteen and forty." She sighs. She is kneeling on the floor next to where Zhang is sitting, looking up at him as if she were his daughter. "So where are you taking me tonight?"

"Nowhere," Zhang says. "I'm here to tell you that the emperor's going to want you tonight."

"Oh, curse the emperor! He's so hairy, and he stinks. Tell me again about this cousin Pei Pei of yours. Tell me again how handsome he is."

Zhang looks down at the girl sitting at his feet and wonders how she is ever supposed to represent an entire province. How could she ever symbolize fifty million people? She is naïve and immature, just like everyone else in Henan. Maybe that's it, he thinks, maybe it takes someone who is naïve to represent those who are also naïve.

"I can't wait until he comes," she continues. "These maids are so boring! They look at you as if you have knives for eyes. I don't have *any* friends here." She looks down.

"What about the other concubines?" Zhang says. "Lady Xiu lives down the hall. Have you tried making her acquaintance yet?"

The girl shakes her head. "I spoke to her once," she says. "She's very secretive. Why are all educated people so secretive? Sometimes she goes out in the middle of the night."

Lady Xiu is the only concubine who has a college degree. At twenty-four, she is also the oldest. She represents Beijing, which the emperor considers a province all to itself. He met her after his siege of the city, when he declared himself emperor and told the Chinese people about his plans for the sexual senate. He saw her at a suburb along the outskirts of the city, where he ordered the town to line up its available girls so he could choose. Right away, he knew he wanted Xiu. She wasn't the most beautiful, but she was the most adamant, speaking confidently and clinging to his arm.

"Nobody knows what she does," Lady Jing continues. "The maids think she has a lover."

"She better hope the emperor doesn't find out." Zhang walks to the door.

"At least she has something to be excited about. I have nothing."

"I'll see to it that my cousin is here within the month," Zhang says, passing through the silk veil.

As he walks back through the palace halls and into the courtyard, he thinks about Pei Pei. "I am doing him a favor," he tells himself. But he doesn't recognize his own voice anymore. "I am fortunate," he says. "Millions of people would love to be in my position." He walks in small, mincing steps—the only way he is able to walk after the operation. He feels useless whenever he walks. "Anyway, I can't take it back now." The only thing he can improve now is his status in the palace. First, he must gain the emperor's full confidence, then surround the emperor with his own allies. If his power continues to grow, he will soon have enough people around him to do anything he wants, perhaps overthrow the emperor and his traditions. *Do to him what he has done to me.* Smiling, he opens the door to his room and claps his hands twice.

"You have to go," Pei Pei's father says. "Zhang tells us it's an order from the emperor. If you don't go, they can have us beheaded."

"Please don't tell Song," Pei Pei says. "I told her that I might be going to the city. She thinks I have a job prospect."

"You are thinking about this situation the wrong way," his father says. "Song will be proud to learn that her husband has achieved a high rank."

His mother nods. "There are many paths that lead to a girl's heart," she says.

"Just don't say a word," Pei Pei says again and shuts the door.

When he gets home, he sees fabric lying around the floor and on the bed and on top of the furnace. Song has an old magazine on her lap and has needles in her mouth.

"What's all this?" Pei Pei asks.

"I went to the store today," she says. "You have to look good for the interview. Come and look at this magazine. Tell me which shirt you want."

"It's not glamorous," Pei Pei says. "I'll just be working for a bicycle route."

"*If* you get it," she corrects him.

"How did you get money for these things?"

"I've been saving up the allowances you gave me," she says. "And I borrowed the rest from my parents."

"You shouldn't have." He walks over and takes the needle and half-sewn fabric out of her hands and puts them on top of the furnace. He puts his hands on her shoulders and moves them slowly down to her breasts and then down to her hips. He kisses her hair. Then he leans over and whispers into her ear, "Come to bed. You can do this in the morning."

She shrugs him off. She reaches over his shoulder and grabs the needle and fabric. "Not tonight," she says. "We have more important things to think about."

He stops touching her. As he walks to the bed, he mumbles, "What's more important than a woman's duty to her husband?" He snuggles onto the hard bed and covers his face with his blanket.

"Pei Pei," Song says, "you shouldn't act like this. We can do it any time you want. Right now, there are more important things. You have to think about *your* duties as well. A man needs to take care of his family."

He doesn't lift the covers. He whispers, and this time soft enough so she can't hear, "What family?"

The imperial palace is surrounded by three rings of walls. A shallow moat surrounds the outer wall. Poorer citizens use its waters to wash their clothes. Three drawbridges, each guarded by a pair of tanks, connect the city to the palace. The emperor understands that the moat and walls are not of any practical use. Rather, they are a symbol of power, rooted in tradition, something to make the Chinese people believe that he has obtained the Mandate of Heaven.

"I've never once seen those drawbridges up before," Zhang says to Pei Pei. They are sitting in his limo. Crowds of people swarm the car, holding signs. They are yelling profanities, demanding change. The driver gets out, shoves his way over to the tanks, and then maneuvers back to the car. A tank comes over and clears a path. They follow it through the outermost wall.

"Who are those people?" Pei Pei asks.

"Young reformers," Zhang says. "They've been protesting since the palace was built. Don't mind them. The emperor is thinking about cleaning them out."

"What do they want?"

"Democracy, mostly. They're not satisfied with the concubine system. They don't see that the concubine system *is* democracy. Instead of asking for more, they should embrace what they have and make grievances to their provincial concubine."

"Would that give them what they want?" Pei Pei asks.

"Not if they want the impossible," Zhang says.

They pass through the outer rings and enter the palace court-

NEW WORK IN NEW CHINA

yard. Winter turns to spring. Pei Pei starts seeing everything as if through a curtain of green silk. Willows and peach trees fill the yard. Women wearing traditional Chinese dresses walk past them holding umbrellas. Pink and orange petals fall from the dome.

They drive up to Zhang's mansion. His chambermaids stand by the door to greet them. A girl takes Zhang's hand and the other one carries Pei Pei's bag.

"You've arrived just when the emperor has departed for the outskirts of Inner Mongolia," Zhang explains. "The emperor is serving double duty on this trip, both to check up on the situation of his forces at the front and also to find an Inner Mongolian concubine."

"What do I do now?" Pei Pei asks, looking around Zhang's mansion. Antiques litter the room beneath giant fans. Unraveled paintings and coiled calligraphy cover the walls. Large decorated vases and tangled ginseng roots sit in the corners. It's as if he's back in ancient times, in one of those pictures he has seen in history books.

"Don't worry," Zhang says. "There are still other people to see. But first we have to get you out of those clothes."

Pei Pei looks down at the shirt Song has made him: a cleverly designed shirt with alternating strips of blue and yellow fabric to make it look like a striped sweater. He thinks about the time it took Song to make it, the time wasted, the time he could have helped her conceive. This shirt might have cost me a son, he thinks. And then he blames himself. If he hadn't been such a coward she wouldn't have wasted that time on something so useless.

That entire night, he can't sleep for thinking about Song. Around two in the morning, a chambermaid walks in and sees his naked body. Pei Pei quickly covers himself. "Tea?" the girl asks, and he suspects she might have forgotten someone was in the guest room. "No, thank you," he says, and she leaves, smiling coyly. He lies back down, feeling pleased that he had such an effect. It's obvious that she hasn't seen a real man for months. If he becomes a eunuch, he will no longer have this effect on any woman. No amount of handsomeness or cleverness can save a man who doesn't have it where it counts.

"When you see Lady Jing," Zhang says, "immediately go to your knees and kowtow three times. Also, always stand a meter or more away, and don't ever touch her. Understand?"

Pei Pei nods. Zhang knocks on the red door, and the chambermaid opens it, taking his hand. Pei Pei follows them inside, almost tripping on his robe, which swings from side to side, trailing the ground. When they pass a silk veil, Pei Pei kneels and starts kowtowing.

"Is this him?" Lady Jing asks. "Stand up. Please, stand up."

Pei Pei gets up, looks at the girl's face for a second, and then looks down again, his chin touching his neck. The girl is beautiful. She smells of bananas and lavender. She wears a large floppy headdress with flickering rubies and sapphires.

"I'd like to be alone with him," she says. She waves her hands and Zhang and the chambermaids exit through the silk veil.

She bounces next to Pei Pei and takes his arm. They sit on the bed for a few minutes not saying anything. Then the girl grabs a bunch of letters off her table and flips through them carelessly.

"Do you know anything about laws?" she asks.

Pei Pei shakes his head.

"Can you read?"

He nods.

"I've been getting these letters incessantly," she says, handing him one. "Read me this one."

NEW WORK IN NEW CHINA

He flips it open. "I'm not a very good reader," Pei Pei confesses. "I stopped going to school when I was fifteen."

"You have a beautiful voice. The emperor reads these letters to me, but he has a thick accent. I fall asleep before he finishes. Go on, read it to me."

Pei Pei holds the letter over the light and squints to make out the handwriting. "Dear Lady Jing," he reads, "we hope you are happy in your new home in Tibet. We wish you a thousand smiles. Our school is located in Xinchun Village. We haven't had a teacher for a while now. Our last teacher, Mr. Bai, became a *gong-gong*. We know that he is needed elsewhere, that by serving the emperor, he is also serving us.

"We understand that the emperor can't afford to send great men, those who graduated from the universities, to come and teach a peasant village. But if someone who is literate can be sent over, we would be grateful. We, the parents, donated our savings and hired a man from the city to help us write our words down in—"

"You can stop now." She yawns. "I'm going to fall asleep. Maybe it wasn't the emperor's accent that made the letters boring."

"There's more," Pei Pei says.

"Never mind," the girl says. "Come here and sit next to me. Zhang tells me you have a wife. Is she pretty? Do you have a picture? Has she given you any children yet?"

Pei Pei puts the letter back on the girl's desk and sits down next to her. He talks but doesn't know what he's saying. He describes what Song looks like, but he can no longer picture her in his head. Children? He doesn't even know if he wants children anymore. How many children does a man need anyway? How many children can the world support? The girl listens with enthusiasm. She likes him. She'll treat his family well here. Song will not need to worry anymore. *He* will not need to worry anymore.

Over the next few days, Pei Pei begins to accept his fate. He spends a great deal of time with Lady Jing, learning the trade. In the afternoon, he accompanies her to the Discussion Room where all the concubines meet with their provincial lobbyists. Lady Jing finds these events boring and always falls asleep. "When you officially become my *gong-gong*," she says to Pei Pei, "I can stay at home and you can take my place."

There are very few concubines who attend these meetings, and the ones who do tend to be indifferent. Their *gong-gongs* speak with the lobbyists for them. Having been to only a few of these meetings, Pei Pei has already noticed the grin on their faces when the lobbyists hand them envelopes, which he suspects are stuffed with money. When he becomes a *gong-gong*, Pei Pei thinks, he will not be so easily corrupted. He will act on behalf of the people and use his position for the benefit of New China.

The only concubine who seems enthusiastic at these meetings is Lady Xiu of Beijing. Her *gong-gong* is never present. She argues with the lobbyists in a refined manner. Instead of allocating money to the big businesses, she distributes the money to schools and orphanages. She has also started a program that helps underprivileged young people in the countryside find jobs in the city. The lobbyists hate her. Watching her argue, Pei Pei finds her a remarkable woman. He would like to join her cause as soon as he comes to power.

A few hours before a meeting, Lady Jing complains of a headache and tells Pei Pei to attend in her place. During the meeting, the Henan lobbyists talk amongst themselves, seeing that Pei Pei is not officially anything yet, and hand him envelopes, telling him to deliver them to Lady Jing. After the meeting, taking advantage of Lady Jing's absence, Pei Pei walks over to Lady Xiu and introduces himself.

"I admire what you're doing," he says. "New China needs more concubines like you."

Lady Xiu looks him up and down, and Pei Pei realizes that he has forgotten his place, that he is not officially anything yet. He kneels and begins to kowtow.

"You still have your testicles?" she asks.

Pei Pei nods. He looks up and sees that she is smiling. Her eyes are surprisingly gentle.

She leans in. "Let me give you some advice," she whispers. "Keep your testicles. Leave this place."

"What does the lady mean?" he asks.

"Come to my chambers and I'll explain."

He follows her down the palace hallway and into her private chambers. Her maids stand guard by the door. Inside, the room is almost identical to Lady Jing's room. The bed, desk, chairs, lamp, and vases are all placed in the same locations. Stacks of books and papers litter the floor. On her desk is a large typewriter with a half-written letter inside.

She sits down and puts on a pair of spectacles. "The emperor doesn't allow us to have televisions or computers," she says, typing the letter. "I had to have my chambermaids steal this typewriter from outside the palace walls."

He looks around and realizes that something is missing. "Why doesn't the Lady have a *gong-gong*?" he asks.

"He sleeps in his room all day. It's what I tell him to do. You can never trust eunuchs. They're always out for themselves. Useless in more than one way."

Pei Pei keeps quiet. With her spectacles on, Lady Xiu doesn't look like a concubine at all; she looks like a young girl in a pretty dress, like a college student hard at work.

"You are from the countryside?" she asks.

"I am," he says. He feels almost ashamed.

She laughs. "You walk in giant steps, like you're standing in a sorghum field."

He looks down. "Is that why Lady Xiu thinks I am not fit to become a *gong-gong*?"

She slides over and takes his hand. "No one is fit to become a *gong-gong*," she says. "Why would you want to give up what you have *for this*? Some of us are here not because we want to be, but because we have to."

"My village is poor," he says. "We have no food. My family is counting on me."

"Your family needs you to be where you are."

Pei Pei nods, and then looks down. "Lady Jing will be wondering why I'm not back yet."

Lady Xiu smiles. She leans in and kisses him on the cheek.

Busy commanding his armies in Mongolia, the emperor has left Zhang in charge of the palace. Before he left, he told Zhang to be especially weary of Lady Xiu. The emperor complained that she had been more interested in politics than in sex during her nights with him. Zhang told the emperor that he was suspicious of her himself. One night, while taking a walk on the outermost walls, he saw her talking with some strange men. She was disguised, but dropped her hood for a moment and Zhang could tell she was a concubine. Her headdress also indicated that she was from Beijing. "If anything else of the slightest suspicion occurs," the emperor said to Zhang, "do not hesitate to take action."

Zhang is pleased that the emperor has given him such powers. He wants to take full advantage of them and appoint Pei Pei before the emperor returns. Secretly, Zhang calls Pei Pei's parents. He tells them to pack their bags and prepare to leave for Tibet. He also tells them to inform Song that her husband will become a high official. Pei Pei has been in Tibet for a week now, and Zhang suspects that he is beginning to get used to the daily baths, meaty meals, and soft beds of palace life.

"It's time to set a date for the operation," he says. "I've spoken to the surgeons. How does next Tuesday sound?"

"Can't we wait until the emperor returns?" Pei Pei asks.

"The emperor has already accepted you," Zhang says. "Anyway, it's better to have the operation before he arrives, in case for some reason he really doesn't want you."

Pei Pei nods. To try and relieve some of his anxieties, Zhang takes him to the room where he is to have the operation. The room, with its stone walls and small windows, reminds Pei Pei of a dungeon. A wooden bed is located at the center, leather straps hanging off the sides. The surgeons who greet them don't look like doctors at all. They are all eunuchs, dressed in yellow and red half-moon jerseys, with strange grins on their faces.

The night before the operation, it snows. Overhead, a sheet of white covers the green panels, barely allowing light to escape through. At noon, the courtyard already has its streetlamps turned on. Pei Pei sits on the steps outside of Zhang's mansion, thinking about tomorrow. He turns around and looks through the window at Zhang, who is laughing and talking on his cell phone. That is what I will become, Pei Pei thinks. He imagines Zhang speaking in his high voice. "I am Zhang Mei," he tries to mimic, but he can't imagine his own voice ever changing into that.

Zhang opens the window. "Your parents want to talk to you!"

Pei Pei gets up and walks into the mansion. "Here he comes," Zhang says, and hands him the phone.

"We're so happy you have made your decision," Pei Pei's mother says.

"Congratulations!" his father says. "But you have to speak with Song. She is hysterical."

Pei Pei looks at Zhang, who smiles back. He carries the phone outside and takes a seat on the steps again.

No one is at the other side of the line anymore. He hears a lot of noise in the background. His parents are having a party. Among the drunken shouts, he hears someone sobbing.

He has never heard Song's voice through a receiver, and he is surprised that he even recognizes it.

"Is this what you want?" she says.

He doesn't say anything.

"How could I have known you were unsatisfied with me? You don't yell at me. You don't hit me. You tell me I'm a good wife. How could I have known?"

Suddenly, everything becomes clear. His parents must have tricked her. He can see their faces. They stare at the fabric and needles and magazines lying around Song's room. "Look at all the stuff you buy," they say. "It's no wonder he feels so much pressure. You're a spendthrift." He can see them going to the furnace and looking through the pot of rice and the stew cooking on top. They take a ladle and have a sip of the stew. Their faces turn sour. "And how can he eat this every day?" they say. "It's really no wonder."

"You have nothing to be ashamed of," Pei Pei says. "I'm coming home."

"We used to be so happy," Song says. "I remember the summertimes when we used to find spots in the wheat fields and we'd hide ourselves from the other workers. I remember the times when we were kids, when you sneaked up to my window and took me to the watermelon fields. We pretended we were husband and wife and the watermelon halves were bowls of rice. You told me you wanted three sons to help you in the fields, and you promised me a daughter."

He can hear her stifled tears. Sitting on the steps, he puts his head in his hands and rubs his face. He looks up at the green panels of glass where the sky is supposed to be and suddenly everything around the courtyard seems dark. Petals fall on his legs and shoulders and face, but because of the layer of snow covering the panels, the petals lose their color and look more like flakes of charcoal landing on his skin.

The snow falls heavier and the palace grows darker. Later that evening, Zhang's spies follow Lady Xiu as she makes her way through the three walls and past the moat. She's wearing a black sweater with a black hood. They see her conferring with several people outside the palace and then giving them a letter. Immediately, Zhang's men try to arrest her. The men around her retaliate against the spies, one of whom is severely wounded. The guards sound the alarm, and because of the flatness of the desert and the footprints on the snow, Lady Xiu and her accomplices are easily captured.

Upon reading the letter, Zhang determines that Lady Xiu has been part of the rebellion all along. She has coordinated plans with the college students to take advantage of the emperor's absence and conspired to storm the palace. In order to demonstrate that treason will not be tolerated, Zhang has decided on the immediate execution of the former lady.

Tuesday morning, as the snow outside accumulates to over thirty centimeters—a Tibetan record—Zhang stands on top of the inner-most palace wall and looks upon the execution. The greenhouse is still dark from the accumulated snow, but the heavy-duty lamps have been turned on and the courtyard looks as if the sun is out. He feels that Lady Xiu's execution is happening at a most opportune time. Pei Pei stands next to him, wearing the striped shirt his wife made for him, his bags packed. He would have left this morning if it hadn't been for the snow.

"What did she do?" Pei Pei asks.

"She was very dumb," Zhang whispers. "If she wanted to over-throw the emperor, she should have waited. Gain his confidence in full and then take action. What did she think she could have accom-plished? The emperor still has his armies."

On the square below, soldiers with ceremonial spears grab Lady Xiu by the arms and drag her through the petal-covered grass and pull her onto a platform. Her hair is wild with a few jasmine pet-als stuck in it, hanging underneath her torn title hat. The two sol-diers bring Lady Xiu to the far side of the platform and tie her to a pole. Below the platform, her chambermaids are also tied up. Next to them, a fire burns with the former Lady's letters and typewriter. One of the soldiers underneath walks up to a chambermaid, takes out his pistol, and shoots her in the head. Then he walks up to the other one and shoots her in the same way.

"Your parents told me about Song's disapproval," Zhang says. "I understand that you are leaving for her sake. It's very noble of you."

The soldiers drop their ceremonial spears and pick up bolt-action rifles. They march to the other side of the platform and look up at Zhang, waiting for a signal. Lady Xiu moves her head around. Strands of hair hide her forehead. Her head is hunched over, weighed down by the torn headdress. She tries to keep it up by pressing it against the pole, but it keeps falling down. Eventually she gives up and her head falls almost to her shoulders.

"After all, what is a man without a woman?" Zhang says. Once Pei Pei crosses over, he will understand. He only needs a push in the right direction. He is still my cousin, Zhang thinks, someone who needs my help. "Except," Zhang continues, "a better, more independent, and clearer-thinking man."

"You should wait until the emperor comes back before you take any action," Pei Pei says.

"Pei Pei," Zhang says. "You misunderstand what New China is about. The emperor is not New China. His time is limited. We are its future."

"Zhang, you can't do this. She is a good woman. She cares about China."

Zhang nods to the soldiers below. They count down from ten. On five, the soldiers shoulder their rifles. On two, they take aim. On one, Lady Xiu's headdress falls to the ground and rolls to the other side of the platform, by the feet of the soldiers.

"Do you understand?" Zhang continues, his long rabbit ears quivering. "*We* are its future. We will be the ones in power once the emperor loses control. These concubines—they're nothing. They're puppets. It's going to be men like us, eunuchs, the most intelligent and most ruthless and most loyal to each other, who will be at the top."

Pei Pei feels dizzy, listening to Zhang's voice. It slides into his ears like a rusted knife and then down into his pants. He can feel everything coming off, everything dropping. He can see the future of New China: thousands of men in his likeness.

"Becoming a *gong-gong*," Zhang says, "is the only path there is."

Pei Pei sees children smiling and clapping their hands twice, sees men of his likeness taking care of them. New China doesn't need more people; it needs to take care of what it already has. It doesn't want him back in the countryside, creating more problems. The country folks watch him. They are counting on him. They chant his name and stare at him with awe. He walks near them, striding like someone in a sorghum field, but they don't seem to recognize him anymore. As he approaches, they draw back. They ask him: *Who are you?*

The young emperor returns from Inner Mongolia triumphantly. His armies have now pushed back the Communists to upper Mongolia and are laying siege to Ulaanbaatar. It should be a matter of weeks before the communist leaders surrender. To celebrate the thorough defeat of his enemy, the emperor has decreed that he will double the number of concubines in his court. In order to represent the people of New China thoroughly, he will need two concubines for every province: just like how it is in America!

Some of his eunuchs, including Zhang, advise the emperor against having more concubines. While it's true the incident with Lady Xiu has shaken the emperor, he believes that the quick and thorough actions of Zhang have proven the court can handle more. From now on, he will no longer accept any girl with a college education. Whereas *gong-gongs* must be intelligent, concubines serve only as a median between the emperor and the people. Any girl with a college education, the emperor reasons, has already separated herself from the general mass, and therefore cannot represent the people accurately. He will choose more girls like Lady Jing, who everyone in the court considers a model concubine.

In order to support these additional concubines, the emperor has to recruit additional *gong-gongs*. There will be a new entrance exam. It will look for intelligence above all else. College graduates are preferable. The emperor instructs his current line of eunuchs to begin development of this exam. Sitting high up on his throne, he claps his hands twice. His eunuchs walk in mincing steps and stand hunched before him. He scans them one by one, nodding his head, inhaling and exhaling like a meditating Buddha. He takes pride in all of his *gong-gong*s, who consider their current station in New China to be most fortunate.

Acknowledgments

The stories in *Further News of Defeat* represent over a decade of writing, and they are possible only with the support of more family, friends, teachers, and colleagues than I can name here. Still, I offer my deepest gratitude to the following people:

I am indebted to the feedback and encouragement of my early teachers at Northwestern University, Anna Keesey and Brian Bouldrey, the pointed guidance of the MFA faculty at Purdue, in particular Sharon Solwitz, Porter Shreve, Patricia Henley, and Bich Minh Nguyen, and the continued support of the creative writing faculty at Florida State, especially Elizabeth Stuckey-French, Mark Winegardner, and Robert Olen Butler.

I would like to also thank everyone who has read and commented on these stories over the years: James Xiao, Chris Arnold, Brian Beglin, Mehdi Okasi, Jake Wolff, Carmen Johnson, and the editors at *New England Review*, *The Greensboro Review*, *Hayden's Ferry Review*, and *Juked*. These stories would not be where they are today if not for your insight and vision. I want to thank the wonderful people at Autumn House Press: Shelby Newsom and Christine Stroud, who have made the publishing process fun, exciting, and enlightening.

Finally, I am forever grateful to my parents, whose stories over the years have shaped many of the pieces in this collection, and to my wife, without whom I would be lost.

About the Author

Michael X. Wang was born in Fenyang, a small coal-mining city in China's mountainous Shanxi Province. He immigrated to the United States when he was six and has lived in ten states and fifteen cities. In 2010, he completed his PhD in Literature at Florida State University. Before that, he received his MFA in Fiction at Purdue. His work has appeared in *New England Review*, *The Greensboro Review*, *Day One*, and *Juked*, among others, and was an AWP Intro Journals Winner in Fiction and been selected as a notable story of the year for *The Best American Short Stories Anthology*. He lives with his wife and pets in Russellville, Arkansas, and is currently an Assistant Professor of English and Creative Writing at Arkansas Tech University.

New and Forthcoming Releases

under the aegis of a winged mind by makalani bandele
WINNER OF THE 2019 AUTUMN HOUSE POETRY PRIZE
SELECTED BY CORNELIUS EADY

Circle / Square by T. J. McLemore
WINNER OF THE 2019 AUTUMN HOUSE CHAPBOOK PRIZE
SELECTED BY GERRY LAFEMINA

Hallelujah Station by M. Randal O'Wain

Grimoire by Cherene Sherrard

Further News of Defeat: Stories by Michael X. Wang
WINNER OF THE 2019 AUTUMN HOUSE FICTION PRIZE
SELECTED BY AIMEE BENDER

Skull Cathedral: A Vestigial Anatomy by Melissa Wiley
WINNER OF THE 2019 AUTUMN HOUSE NONFICTION PRIZE
SELECTED BY PAUL LISICKY

No One Leaves the World Unhurt by John Foy
WINNER OF THE 2020 DONALD JUSTICE PRIZE
SELECTED BY J. ALLYN ROSSER

In the Antarctic Circle by Dennis James Sweeney
WINNER OF THE 2020 AUTUMN HOUSE RISING WRITER PRIZE
SELECTED BY YONA HARVEY

Creep Love by Michael Walsh

The Dream Women Called by Lori Wilson

For our full catalog please visit: http://www.autumnhouse.org